MAMA TANDOORI

Ernest van der Kwast is a Dutch author born in
Mumbai, India, in 1981. He made his debut in
2005 with the novel *Sometimes Things Are Better
When People Applaud*. His breakthrough book is
Mama Tandoori, which became a bestseller in the
Netherlands and Italy upon publication, and has to
date sold more than 100,000 copies. It is the second
of his novels (after *The Ice-Cream Makers*) to be
published in English. He lives in Rotterdam.

Ernest van der Kwast

MAMA
Tandoori

TRANSLATED FROM DUTCH BY
LAURA VROOMEN

SCRIBE
Melbourne • London

Scribe Publications
18–20 Edward St, Brunswick, Victoria 3056, Australia
2 John St, Clerkenwell, London, WC1N 2ES, United Kingdom

First published in Dutch by De Bezige Bij 2010
First published in English by Scribe 2017

Typeset in Dante MT 12.6/16.5 by the publishers
Printed and bound in the UK by CPI Group (UK) Ltd, Croydon CR0 4YY

Scribe Publications is committed to the sustainable use of natural resources
and the use of paper products made responsibly from those resources.

9781925322293 (Australian paperback)
9781911344353 (UK paperback)
9781925548334 (e-book)

The publisher gratefully acknowledges the support
of the Dutch Foundation for Literature.

N **ederlands**
letterenfonds
dutch foundation
for literature

CiP records for this title are available from the British Library and the
National Library of Australia.

scribepublications.com.au
scribepublications.co.uk

CONTENTS

TWO SUITCASES

It all began with two suitcases. In 1969, my mother arrived in the Netherlands with two suitcases filled with bangles, necklaces, and earrings. She got a job as a nurse and moved into a room in a nurses' hostel. She hid the suitcases under her bed, which is the best place to keep valuables — according to Indians, that is. My mother once confided in me: 'Burglars never look under beds.' Then my father whispered in my ear: 'In India, hardly anyone actually owns a bed.'

The two suitcases remained under my mother's bed for years, until my father, an awkward man with protruding ears and as Dutch as can be, fell in love with the exotic woman he thought my mother was. I don't know the exact course of events, and to be honest I don't really want to know either, but suffice to say that at some point the suitcases moved to a small house on Bloemstraat, where they ended up under a double bed.

My father was studying medicine and spent all day with his nose — and protruding ears — in a book. My mother worked as a nurse and brought home the bacon. Or in her case, the naan bread. As my mother confided in me: 'Your father was as poor as a rat in Delhi.' And my father whispered in my ear: 'If only I were a rat in Delhi.'

The house on Bloemstraat had paper-thin walls, and was even smellier than my father's armpits. That, at any rate, is what my mother tells me. It can't be verified anymore. The houses on Bloemstraat have all been demolished. A colossal block of flats now stands on the site where my parents once lived. Time's a terrible glutton, an insatiable omnivore. That said, the smell of my father's armpits has never been gobbled up; it seems to be undying. My mother puts it down to his job. My father is a pathologist.

'What's that I smell?' my mother would often ask at the table.

'Mmm,' my father would say. 'Tandoori chicken.'

My mother: 'I smell corpses! The stench of the dead is spoiling my appetite.'

My father brought his nose to his plate. 'Delicious,' he said. 'Tandoori chicken.'

'It's coming from your armpits,' my mother roared. 'That cadaverous smell comes from your armpits! You ought to press your arms against your body!'

Whenever I think of the old days, I see my father sitting at the head of the table, his arms pressed tightly against his body, cutlery dangling clumsily from his hands. As a child, I never visited my father at work, scared I might find him up to his armpits in a corpse.

That noisy, subsided, smelly house on Bloemstraat wasn't the kind where you want to hang around. Before long, my parents went in search of new accommodation. My mother found it on Jericholaan, in the upmarket Rotterdam neighbourhood of Kralingen. Number 81 was a three-storey townhouse with a spacious garden and a tenant, Mr Gerritsen. I never had the pleasure of meeting Mr Gerritsen, though. By the time I was born, he'd already fled the house, shrieking at the top of his lungs: 'She's the devil! She's the devil!'

The house on Jericholaan cost a fortune, but my mother haggled over the asking price, the way she haggled over everything: clothes, furniture, whitegoods, and chicken fillets. Haggling was a hobby — a sport, even. I spent half my childhood in shops and department stores, waiting for the salesperson to give in and reduce the price. I remember a bed store where my mother told the salesman: 'In India, you can buy a hundred bunkbeds for that kind of money.' I didn't say that there are no bunkbeds in India. I did as I was told. I lay stretched out on a mattress and wouldn't get up until my mother signalled for me to do so. This finally happened at half-past four in the afternoon, more than six hours after we'd first entered the store. The salesman looked as if he'd just come out of a twelve-round boxing match. My mother had a triumphant grin on her face. She'd managed to knock 80 per cent off the original price.

The estate agent charged with selling the house on Jericholaan was brought to his knees, too. The story goes that my mother wanted to trade the two suitcases for the house. The estate agent didn't get it. 'You can only pay with money,' he said, whereupon my mother flew into a rage. 'You're insulting me,' she yelled. 'In India, you'd be able to buy an entire town for these suitcases!'

As the estate agent looked at the cases, deep furrows appeared in his forehead, and he began to look more and more despondent. Maybe he was thinking of changing jobs. I reckon that people whose paths crossed my mother's were bound to conclude they'd taken a wrong turn somewhere.

My mother interpreted the agent's silence as interest. She started listing the jewellery that was allegedly in the suitcases: nose rings, ankle chains, bangles, earrings, necklaces, even a golden crown.

The agent glanced helplessly at my father, but he knew he had a speaking ban. All my dad was allowed to do was breathe and nod. (The latter obviously only in response to things my mother said.)

The agent plucked up the courage to mention the asking price. My mother shook her head, divided the asking price in two, subtracted 10,000, compared that price to rupees, divided the figure in two again, and then revealed the outcome.

My father managed to catch the agent as he fell, and whispered in his ear: 'It'll be fine, it'll all be fine. Count yourself lucky: you're not married to her.'

Many more viewings followed, and during each one my mother tried to bring the asking price down. The agent no longer fainted, but after each viewing he had to have a breather on the stone steps in front of the house. He, too, must have looked as if he'd just survived a twelve-round boxing match.

In the end, my mother sold the contents of the two suitcases to Rotterdam's top jewellers. With the proceeds, she bought Number 81 Jericholaan.

Those who doubt this transaction had better have good reflexes. They can expect a clobbering with a rolling pin. It wasn't uncommon in my childhood for roti to be off the menu because the rolling pin was broken again. Likewise, I remember my father with an ice pack on his head, muttering: 'If only I were a rat in Delhi; If only I were a rat in Delhi …'

On Jericholaan, there were no more suitcases under my parents' bed. They had made way for other valuable items, such as an inherited microscope and bales of basmati rice. By now my father had graduated and was earning an income as a junior doctor. His salary, according to my mother, equalled that of a porter at Bombay station.

Bombay (as it was then called): my birthplace.

It remains a mystery to me why my two brothers were born in the Netherlands, whereas I was born in India, and why my father was in Rotterdam while my mother gave birth to me in Bombay. Personally, I think it may have had something to do with a special deal. Bargains truly are irresistible to my mother, like a red rag to a bull.

This is the scenario that comes to mind: *Air India* allows children to travel for free, making the offer for the outbound flight three for the price of one — and for the inbound flight, four for the price of one. But that meant my father had to stay at home. And so he did, quite possibly on my mother's orders.

Shortly after I emerged from my mother's belly, Uncle Sharma phoned my father. He ended up thinking I was a girl. 'There were little birds on the line,' my father whispered in my ear one day, shortly after my mother confided in me that my father is stone deaf and only hears what he wants to hear. '*Deodorant* is a word your father never hears. *Soap* is another word your father never hears. *Could you please take a shower* is a sentence your father never, ever hears.'

But I digress. Let us return to the two suitcases. They'd assumed the shape of an impressive townhouse in Kralingen. My parents lived on the ground and first floors, while Mr Gerritsen occupied the attic. This went well, until my mother discovered the concept of 'rent control'. It slipped out of Mr Gerritsen's mouth. My mother exploded. 'Rent control?' she exclaimed, making it sound like a nasty venereal disease. 'Get out of my house. Quick, out of my house!' But Mr Gerritsen stayed — for another three days, to be precise.

On day one, my mother burned black rubbish bags in the back garden. As the sky filled with thick smoke, she shrieked: 'Be gone, spirit! Evil spirit of Mr Gerritsen, be gone!' In addition, she got up at three in the morning to bang a broom against the ceiling while uttering a traditional text people in India recite when someone is terminally ill.

On day two, my mother went to the petting zoo in Kralingse Bos, on the outskirts of town, and stole cow manure. She was almost caught in the act, because she was determined to get the freshest manure. A child raised the alarm: 'Mummy! Mummy! That lady is putting Bella's poop into her bag.' Back home, my mother donned her rubber gloves and began baking biscuits for the upstairs neighbour.

On day three, Mr Gerritsen suffered with diarrhoea and my mother switched off the water mains. She also banged her broom nonstop against the ceiling while reciting the aforementioned traditional text.

On day four, my mother prepared a festive meal to thank the Hindu gods for Mr Gerritsen's sudden departure.

And so the value of the two suitcases increased to a townhouse minus a tenant.

My parents lived on Jericholaan for ten years, but the family wouldn't expand any further. My mother had stopped working because she had her hands full raising three sons. My father had qualified as a regular doctor and now earned the salary of 'a rickshaw puller in Bangalore'.

I had a happy childhood, but perhaps only because I didn't know any better. Perhaps I was too young to grasp what was happening around me. I thought we were a normal family, that every household had a mother like my mother, and a father who muttered, 'If only I were a rat.' If not in Delhi, then in Rotterdam, Deventer, or Goes.

My eldest brother has learning disabilities. He's the only one who still thinks it's normal for fathers to sit at the table with their arms pressed against their body, for rubbish bags to be burned in the garden, and for estate agents to be attacked with a rolling pin. The latter happened when the house on Jericholaan was sold, a decade after my parents had moved into Number 81.

My mother had set her sights on a better place: a detached house with a garage, a patio, and a view of Kralingse Plas, a lake. 'We can't afford it,' my father said, to which my mother immediately replied: '*You* can't afford it.'

My mother's plan was to sell the place on Jericholaan at a profit and invest the equity in the detached house. She'd engaged a new estate agent.

The one who'd sold them Jericholaan probably worked as a librarian by then, in dead silence, among row upon row of books.

The new agent described the price my mother wanted for Jericholaan as 'disproportional'. At first it appeared as if my mother was unfamiliar with the word, that when she disappeared from the living room perhaps it was because she went to look it up in a dictionary, but when she re-entered the room she had a rolling pin in her hand. 'Disproportional,' she shouted, as if this too was a venereal disease. 'Get out of my house!'

My father added: 'Run!'

The agent jumped up from his chair and fled to the front door.

My eldest brother chanted: 'Go, mum. Go, mum!'

My other brother and I were shamed into silence. By now we knew we weren't a normal family.

When the agent failed to return, my mother decided to sell the house herself. And so it happened that every week we witnessed another person fleeing the house. As a young girl, my mother had been a promising athlete. Her bedside table boasted large trophies. And while the cups had become dull and rusty, my mother's legs remained quick as a bullet. At the age of 40, she could still sprint like the devil. Occasionally, she'd catch a potential buyer and burst into her usual lament: 'For that money, you can't even buy a sheet of corrugated iron in India.'

The carpet in the hallway was beginning to show signs of wear and tear when one day an elderly gentleman offered a price my mother could live with. Two different versions of that price have been passed down: my father's and my mother's. And since the latter was always right, the price was twice as high as the asking price. My mother has a lot in common with Willem Frederik Hermans. The celebrated Dutch author was always right, too, and he also had flaming rows about money, not with estate agents but with publishers. I remember reading his correspondence about an advance. Hermans' publisher at De Bezige Bij, Geert Lubberhuizen, had written a letter saying: 'I only removed one zero.' My mother would have known what to do with that response. She'd have forced her way into the publisher's headquarters in Amsterdam and beaten that zero back into Mr Lubberhuizen's head.

The detached house was purchased. A friend of my mother's moved us in with his blue van. Professional removal companies were too expensive; in fact, they didn't even exist in India. And so a little old van made 37 trips between Jericholaan and Tiberiaslaan.

Over the years, my mother had become a compulsive hoarder. With the dedication of a Salvation Army major, she devoted herself to taking in bulky waste. The things other people dumped by the side of the road — broken radios, rusty bikes, tattered furniture — she dragged back to Jericholaan. One day she'd take it all to India and delight people over there;

that was my mother's dream. She was convinced that the poor, the pariahs, the people with nothing but their bodies, are happy with anything — even a television without a screen.

My mother's distant past is a dark stain. I know little about it; shame keeps her mouth firmly buttoned. But sometimes she wakes at night from a dream about a beggar's life, many, many years ago. As a scream breaks open her mouth, the darkness of the night provides comfort, a hundred times lighter than the dark stain of her early memories.

From behind their blinds, the residents of Tiberiaslaan watched the moving-in process anxiously. To them, the blue van must have looked like an inverted refuse truck. Again and again, new loads of household effects were dumped outside the house. Before long, a mountain of electronic equipment, bicycles, and furniture had sprung up — a mountain that was still there the following day, at the crack of dawn. By now, the move had gone on for more than 28 hours. And after each trip my father roared: 'I'm never moving house again.'

My parents would move a further three times, or two and a half, to be precise.

On the day my debut novel came out, 24 February 2005, my parents announced they were emigrating to Canada. My father had been offered a job in Toronto. According to my mother, the salary was considerably better — average, by Indian standards.

My parents travelled to Toronto royal-family style: on separate planes. Not that royalty had anything to do with it, though. It just took my mother three months to pack everything. While my father was living and working across the ocean, my mother spent day and night preparing to move her hoard. During the day, she'd cycle to supermarkets around Rotterdam and pick up empty boxes. At night, those boxes were filled. What had once contained jam, coffee, or fruit now held an accumulation of rubbish, ranging from discarded phones to worn bike saddles.

My mother had left India with two suitcases; for her move to Canada, she couldn't even make do with two containers. The relocation had all the hallmarks of a massive provisioning process, of an army being supplied with provisions.

My father welcomed my mother in their new but temporary home: an apartment in a neighbourhood populated predominantly by men in leather trousers. My father hadn't been allowed to buy a house himself. My mother didn't think he was capable of it. And so he'd sought refuge in rented accommodation.

'Among the homosexuals,' my mother exclaimed.

'It's cheap,' replied my father, who'd come to think of himself as dirt poor. It was the easy version of his life. *Once upon a time, his wife had arrived from India laden with jewels. She bought a house, followed by another, and yet another. Meanwhile, he earned the salary of a tailor in Bhopal ...* This version provided peace and quiet, so my father, like other men, could sit on the couch and read his paper without getting assaulted with a rolling pin.

In next to no time, my mother found a new house, on Bloor Street, in the grand Rosedale condominium complex (complete with swimming pool, fitness room, and library). The move caused congestion in front of the four lifts that were used all day to ferry boxes up to the 23rd floor. An elderly lady asked my mother if she was opening a supermarket. The caretaker was less naïve and immediately recognised what type of woman my mother was: the type you want to get away from.

George was a little old man with horn-rimmed glasses, who spent the livelong day behind the reception of the condominium complex. His job was to greet the residents ('Good morning, Miss Henderson!' 'Have a nice day, Mr Glennon!'), and answer the phone once in a blue moon. It was George's dream job. He could remain seated all day, and so time would pass and take him gently towards retirement. But then my mother entered George's life. Like all Rosedale residents, she paid a service charge, but she was alone in concluding that this made the caretaker a *servant*, of the kind you might find in well-to-do households in India. In other words, a kind of glorified slave.

'*Georrrrge*,' my mother would bark non-stop. 'Could you pick up those banana boxes and bring them to my apartment?' Or: 'My flowers are dying;

don't forget to water them today.' Or: 'Please, my husband *really* needs deodorant.'

And so George would hide as soon as my mother's voice boomed through the marble lobby. There were other caretakers, but my mother would only ever ask them, 'Do you know where George is?' To which those caretakers replied that he'd be back in the afternoon, or the evening.

Harsh winters and long summers passed. And then George received what may have been the best news of his life: that my parents were moving house. George was hiding under the counter when he heard my mother tell a neighbour: 'We're moving.' She listed the benefits of the new condominium: two bathrooms, higher ceilings, a sunroom. George leapt up and tears came to his eyes when my mother said: 'Of course, we'll miss George terribly …'

After three years in Rosedale, my mother thought the time had come to move again. She'd spotted a luxury condominium under construction, not far from Mount Sinai Hospital. My father would be able to walk to work. Right now, he cycled 20 minutes to and from work every day, braving the traffic of a metropolis — even in snowy conditions or at –15 degrees Celsius. (My mother had stolen the bike from the Rosedale garage. Parked there were two abandoned bicycles, their saddles covered in a thick layer of dust: one for my mother, one for my father. With my eyes closed, I can picture a lock being opened with a file. My father is keeping a lookout, muttering, praying to all the Indian gods: 'Please restore my wife's common sense.' My mother pays no notice and carries on filing. She's not doing anything wrong, just taking care of two bikes. And when I open my eyes again, I see these words written down. I hope I'm not doing anything wrong either; I'm just taking care of my parents.)

While George was starting to feel better by the day, my parents spent time with the project developer, selecting the marble for their bathrooms, the wood flooring, the colour of the walls. Likewise, the kitchen could be designed to their specifications, to include anything from a granite or a metal kitchen counter to red cabinets or cupboards the colour of lemon. Four months later, when their brand-spanking-new apartment on the fortieth floor was completed, it would all be installed.

But the move never happened. The various reasons given were that the living room was too small, the swimming pool in the complex had no windows, and nearly all the neighbours were Chinese. Not that my mother has any particular issues with Chinese people. She only has issues with people who don't understand her — a number that easily surpasses the entire population of China.

The real reason was that my mother deemed the move too expensive. The *transport exceptionnel* from Rotterdam to Toronto had been paid for by my father's employer. The move within Toronto was at their own expense. My mother couldn't get rid of the keys to the new apartment fast enough when she saw the prices of several accredited removal companies. The expression 'penny wise and pound foolish' perfectly captures my mother's practices — and only deepens my father's tragic fate.

Luckily for my parents, their apartment in Rosedale hadn't yet been sold. George, however, was inconsolable. He collapsed when my mother told him: 'I've got such good news. We're not moving, after all.' George had to stay in hospital for a week before he was declared fit to go back to work. That said, he never became his old self again.

Meanwhile, my mother went in search of a new estate agent. She refused to have anything more to do with the agent who'd been tasked with selling their apartment in Rosedale. There's no such thing as Indian logic.

It didn't take her long to find a new estate agent; not so a buyer. In the United States, the first few newspaper articles started appearing about people unable to pay their mortgages, and my mother's asking price was 100,000 Canadian dollars above the original. 'It's the only condominium in this complex that's for sale,' my mother argued. The agent gulped and then looked at my father, but his speaking ban remained in place.

Miracle of miracles, the apartment was sold after seven months. A millionaire from Shanghai bought it for his daughter. In the not-too-distant future, she'd be walking across the walnut floor that my parents had chosen, open the red kitchen cabinets that matched pots and pans they'd never use, and drip water onto the grey marble of the bathroom of which my father had always dreamed.

And so the value of the two suitcases rose yet again — by 100,000 dollars, this time.

There followed one more condominium viewing — a solo viewing by my mother. While in Europe for work, my father came to visit me in Italy. He held his grandson in his arms for the first time. And the grandson was sick all over his grandfather for the first time. 'It's the smell of corpses,' my mother said over the phone. My father whispered in his grandchild's ear: 'Never marry an Indian woman, and you'll live a long and happy life.'

My son — six weeks old and with hands like starfish — was all eyes. In his innocence, he'd forget everything he heard and saw. But one day I'd tell him about his grandma, who thought a plane ticket to come and marvel at her first grandchild was too expensive, but did go and view a penthouse with an estate agent. 'She's got her eye on something new,' my father said over dinner. His arms were relaxed, but the cutlery still dangled clumsily from his hands. 'The asking price is three million dollars.'

I closed my eyes and pictured my mother, parking her stolen bike against the wall of a condominium complex before bending down to remove the elastic that protects her trousers from the chain. Inside, in the gleaming entrance lobby, the estate agent is waiting for her. She quickly slips the elastic into her coat pocket and shakes his hand. A little later they're in the lift, whizzing up. The agent opens the door to the penthouse, revealing a sea of space. My mother enters. And at the very top of the condominium complex and at the height of the credit crisis, she views the bathrooms, the bedrooms, the designer kitchen, and the living room with a view across Lake Ontario.

Much has been said about the contents of the two suitcases — the gems, the bangles, the necklaces, and the earrings — but nobody ever laid eyes on them.

'Gorgeous,' my mother says.

THE LAST MOUTH

My mother has graced the front page of a newspaper twice, and very nearly a third time. The first occasion my mother made the paper was in 1966, three years before she came to the Netherlands. *The Times of India* printed a picture of several nurses gathered around the deathbed of a famous film star. One of those nurses was my mother. Or rather: one of the grey blurs was my mother. The paper had lost its colour, the photo its sharpness. What remained was a large black stain (the film star) and various grey dots (six or seven gorgeous Indian nurses). This edition of *The Times of India* was kept in a bank safety deposit box.

Occasionally my mother would retrieve the paper from that box and show it off to visitors. In fact, people visiting us could be divided into two groups: those who didn't get to see the front page of *The Times of India*, and those who were expected to scrutinise the front page of *The Times of India* as though it were a sacred image. Not infrequently, visitors would point to the wrong collection of grey dots, thinking it was her, but my mother never corrected anyone. She was too proud.

I knew which set of dots represented my mother. Once, inside the bank safety deposit room, she'd whispered in my ear: 'You see those luminous grey dots? That's me. I'm holding Prithviraj Kapoor's hand.' My mother was the collection of dots standing closest to the film star's bed.

The other front page that showed my mother was carefully hidden from visitors. I only saw the evening paper in question the day it landed on our doormat: Thursday 12 December 1996. It was a cold, bright day, as I remember it. The wind was sharp as a scythe. People were skating on Kralingse Plas. I had borrowed our neighbour's speed skates and pretended to be a champion skater. My mother and my eldest brother had watched from the side of the pond. My eldest brother can't skate, and he's none too good at reading, writing, arithmetic, or telling time, either. What he's good at is sneezing — when he has a sneezing fit, that is.

On 12 December 1996, my eldest brother had a sneezing fit. Every couple of seconds his nose seemed to explode; and every other minute a foghorn bellowed across Kralingse Plas, as my brother blew his nose on the sleeve of his coat.

I remember the occasion when my brother had a sneezing fit in a restaurant just as the main course was served: tacos with beans and sour cream. If we went out for a meal, it was always the same Mexican restaurant we'd go to — Popocatepetl in the old harbour. Before we left the house, each one of us had to drink half a litre of tap water, because we weren't allowed to order anything to drink at Popocatepetl. My mother thought that drinks prices in restaurants were disproportionally high. For the price of a single glass of Coke you could buy two one-and-a-half-litre bottles in the supermarket — or even three, if it was on special. When the waiter appeared at our table and asked if we wanted something to drink to start with, we had to chant 'no' in unison. And that included my father. My mother thought the food was expensive too, but then there's no avoiding that in restaurants.

In Popocatepetl, the restaurant of my childhood, my eldest brother succumbed to a terrible sneezing fit. The waiter had just wished us 'bon appétit' when the snot went flying and landed on the tacos.

'You can't taste it,' my mother said, and simply carried on eating.

My eldest brother took a bite, too, but sneezed, and out it flew again.

My father lost his patience. 'Stop it,' he snapped. 'Stop it.'

'It's not me who's doing it,' said my brother, the one who's no good at reading, writing, arithmetic, and telling time. 'It's doing it by itself,' he said, and pointed to his body.

❈

My mother had seen the photographer coming. He'd been prowling around them like a predator circling its prey. 'A brown-skinned lady,' my mother said, brandishing Thursday's paper. 'He wanted to photograph a brown-skinned lady in the snow!'

'Vincent Mentzel,' my father said proudly. 'None other than Vincent Mentzel took a photograph of you!'

'Who?'

'Vincent Mentzel. He's photographed the Queen as well.'

'When I get my hands on Vincent Mentzel,' my mother shouted, 'I'll whack him over the head with my rolling pin.'

The issue was this: my mother wasn't dressed for a photo. My mother is petite and extremely thrifty, and she was wearing clothes that were practically disintegrating. In *My Jerusalem,* the Israeli writer Meir Shalev writes: 'The laundry was done in the shower water, the laundry water was used to mop the floor, and the water that had mopped the floor was used to water the garden.' The clothes my mother wore on 12 December 1996 had been worn by my eldest brother and by my middle brother before I got to wear them out in playgrounds and sandpits. My mother graced the front page of *NRC Handelsblad* dressed in rags you'd expect to see on a homeless person. And my eldest brother? He was pictured with snot on his chin, snot on his coat, and snot on his mittens.

'How can I still show my face around here?' my mother despaired. We were living on Tiberiaslaan in Kralingen: everybody here read *NRC Handelsblad*. Everybody had seen my mother, the brown-skinned lady in rags. She was the woman my mother didn't want to be, but sometimes was, because the force of the past can be overwhelming. Poverty, war, and nine older brothers and sisters had certainly put their stamp on my mother's character.

'I was the last mouth,' she once told me, continuing in a whisper about Muslims occupying the region where her family lived. My mother was the tenth child, born during a difficult time. When she was only three weeks old, the family was forced to flee. My mother's mother was so anxious that her breasts stopped producing milk. The last mouth sought food, but found none — not a drop. My newborn mother's life was saved by a small goat. Her eldest sister took her to this goat, where several times a day she drank greedily of the milk that flowed from its udder. 'Pucha' was my mother's nickname, the name given to her by her nine older brothers and sisters. Pucha: after the sound her mouth made at the goat's teat. *Pucha-pucha-pucha*. It's a story that haunts me, that tells me where I'm from, too.

Years later I was photographed by Vincent Mentzel for De Parade, a touring theatre festival. As part of a literary programme that stopped at cities including Rotterdam, The Hague, Utrecht, and Amsterdam, I'd be reading from my work all summer. Slowly, as the camera clicked and flashed, a smile formed on my lips.

'Great,' Mentzel said. 'Nice, natural.'

I was thinking of my mother, her rolling pin at the ready.

And then there's the front page my mother narrowly missed. This time the newspaper was a little more modest — neither of *NRC Handelsblad* or *The Times of India* stature. It was *De Ster van Kralingen*, a free weekly paper delivered to our neighbourhood. It featured reports on local centenarians and missing cats, but also lots of ads from grocery stores and butchers, spreading the word about discounts and bargains. It was my mother's favourite paper. Every week, she devoured it.

The contested front page of *De Ster* boasted a photo of a white woman on an old-style granny bike with heavy shopping bags dangling from the handlebars. The woman in question is Ans de Ruiter, the final customer of Den Toom, a small, local supermarket. It had been in business for 30 years, but having fallen foul of the big takeover machine, it was due to be converted into an Albert Heijn, the latest outpost of a large supermarket chain. The shop had a closing-down sale, with lots of special deals and cut-price offers.

De Ster accompanied the photo with a brief interview with the white woman, mostly about the contents of the bags dangling from the handlebars.

De Ster: 'What did you buy?'

Ans de Ruiter: 'As much as possible.'

There was another woman just like my mother.

'Poor Mr De Ruiter,' my father mumbled.

At the end of the interview, my mother was mentioned. The article said that my mother had been buying her groceries at Den Toom for more than 20 years, that everybody in the supermarket knew her, from the shelf-stackers to the cashiers, and that she'd dearly wanted to be the last customer. But someone else had that honour.

Ans de Ruiter.

When this newspaper hit our doormat, my mother began swearing in Indian. Although I don't speak the language fluently, I can *swear* in Hindi with ease. My mother only ever wanted the best for our future, so she always spoke Dutch to us — sometimes even with the rolling 'r' affected by our neighbours. But whenever the social brakes came off, my mother would erupt in a deluge of Indian swearwords. Who knows, perhaps my brothers and I were the only children in the world who knew ten Indian words for *bastard son*, but who were unable to ask *where's the toilet?* in Hindi.

That good future is happening now. My clothes haven't been worn before, and I'll always be able to fill my mouth. And yet it's as if this future isn't good enough, and will never be good enough. I haven't lived up to my mother's expectations. I'm not a doctor, a lawyer, or an accountant — someone to be mentioned in conversation with neighbours.

When it all becomes too much for my mother and tears roll down her cheeks, she mutters: 'My eldest son has learning disabilities, and my youngest son is a writer.'

Later that same afternoon, the front page of *De Ster van Kralingen* was burnt at the stove. I could hear my mother chant an Indian spell. The rest of the paper was saved and would be pored over later, in search of bargains.

'She hid,' said my mother after she'd disposed of the ashes in the neighbours' garden. 'She waited until I was at the checkout with my trolley, until all of my items were on the belt, until I got a receipt pressed into my palms.'

Ans de Ruiter — a primary-school teacher, as *De Ster* reported — was in my mother's eyes a cheat, someone who'd wrongfully become Den Toom's last customer. My mother should have been the last, nobody else. No one but she should have graced the front page of the local paper. On the supermarket's last day, she'd gone shopping every hour. She kept going back on her bike, brimming with enthusiasm, returning home laden with heavy bags dangling from her handlebars. The kitchen cupboards were overflowing with food and household articles. My father began knocking together a new cupboard, but he couldn't keep pace with my mother's compulsive shopping. Nothing's a match for my mother's compulsive shopping. If something's on special, she can't leave it on the shelf. It's an urge stronger than herself, an addiction that screams out for instant gratification. Once she came home with cat food, although we had neither cat nor kitten. My mother's famous words: 'It was on special.'

My father refused to have the consignment of cat food in the house. 'We've got a guinea pig,' he shouted. But my mother took no notice. A guinea pig would be happy to eat rabbit and tuna. But Raj — after the Bollywood actor my mother had nursed — wouldn't go anywhere near the mashed rabbit in his cage; the guinea pig flatly refused to consume his new food. It earned him a thundering sermon on enduring war and nine older brothers and sisters, and worse: rations of a single lettuce leaf a week.

In the end we gave the tins of cat food to family, friends, and acquaintances. We took one with us to every birthday party to which we'd been invited — wrapped in pretty tissue paper, of course. The reactions varied hugely: from surprised to indignant, from speechless to deeply, deeply disappointed. The upshot was that we received fewer and fewer birthday invites.

On Den Toom's last opening day, just about the entire shop was on special. If Pakistan decided to start a nuclear war, we'd be able to survive for months, if not years, on our supplies.

Since she had her eye on a special that she couldn't carry home on her own, my mother wanted me to come along on her umpteenth trip to Den Toom. I feared the worst, but I knew 'no' wasn't an option. People who are addicted to specials don't take no for an answer — or not my mother, anyway. A refusal would send sparks flying in her brain, and the consequences would be dire.

In the supermarket, my mother pointed to a pallet of chocolate wafers. In an attempt to reassure me, she said: 'We can put them in bags and boxes.' I felt anything but reassured. I wanted to run off, as fast as my legs would carry me. But my mother said: 'Hurry, or other people will beat us to it.'

What other people, I wanted to ask. What other people want to buy a pallet full of chocolate wafers just because they happen to be on special? Those people either don't exist, or they're locked away in a secure unit.

My mother began transferring the wafers to her shopping trolley. Keen to avoid a scene, I followed suit. People were all eyes. It was something of a miracle that my mother didn't feel any shame at such moments. Vincent Mentzel could shoot an entire roll of film without having to fear for his life. It was the past, I thought to myself, the crushing memory of the hunger years, the poverty, war, ten mouths. It wasn't my mother who was doing this; it was doing it by itself. A force that can't be stopped, a force of nature, like an erupting geyser.

And so we wheeled two shopping trolleys chock-full of wafers to the checkout. The cashier who knew my mother didn't bat an eyelid. 'Good day, Mrs Van der Kwast,' she said with a friendly smile. 'I see you're back again.'

She scanned pack after pack after pack of wafers. And once all the packs had been scanned, a total appeared on the till display. With a push of a button, the total amount was halved. My mother heaved a sigh of relief.

That same evening, Raj's cage was opened. My mother's hand squeezed in and put down a stack of chocolate wafers. This time there was no need for a sermon. Raj nibbled the wafers as if his life depended on it — and maybe it did. The single lettuce-leaf ration hadn't done him any favours.

By then, the doors of Den Toom had closed for good. The photographer of *De Ster van Kralingen* had taken a picture of Ans de Ruiter. The reporter had promised my mother he'd mention her name in the piece, and write that she'd gone grocery shopping at Den Toom for more than 20 years, that everybody knew her, and that she would have loved to have been the last customer.

Unfortunately, we can't always be who we want to be. More often than not we're that other person, the shadow, the invisible, the lost hope. And if we ever escape our destiny, we slowly morph into grey dots that nobody recognises.

A GIFT FROM GOD

Before my mother got to know my father, before she got on a plane to the Netherlands, before she packed two large suitcases with bangles, necklaces, and earrings, before all that, she looked after the captain of a ship. His name was Rajesh Mudgal. He was his family's eldest son and had thick, dark hair that gleamed in the sunshine.

The captain had fallen ill on the Arabian Sea. The nearest coast was 36 hours' sailing away. Upon his return to shore, Rajesh Mudgal was covered in lumps. He spent a day on the operating table at Bombay hospital. His life was saved, but at a cost: three toes on his right foot, the fingertips of his right hand, and his left leg up to the knee. Rajesh Mudgal would never captain a ship again; he would never sail the seas again.

As soon as the captain was strong enough, he returned home. A special compartment had been reserved for him on the train to Agra, where his parents lived in the gently rolling hills; where he had been born and raised. That night, on the jolting train, Rajesh Mudgal experienced his first phantom pains and screamed until sunrise.

The sight of his native soil brought tears to his eyes. He saw the trees, the houses, and the roads of his childhood; he saw the land he'd swapped for the sea, the dust for the waves. His mother uttered a cry that flew across the hills like a bird. Children gathered around the stretcher and gawped at the dark-blue uniform with the copper buttons, the beautiful trousers that had been mutilated with a pair of scissors. Days of prayer followed.

And then one morning my mother turned up among the trees, the houses, and the roads of dust. She was a white apparition in the sun, a nurse with a crackling aura. With her youth, beauty, and innocence, she entered the house of the Mudgal family, a large, bright home. The family was rich. Father Mudgal was a judge, a man with a voice of stone, each word heavy as a rock. My mother drank tea with the patient's mother. It was quiet; this was a house of sorrow. You could hear a tear drop. Then my mother was taken to the patient. She scrutinised him, seeing his dark, gleaming hair, the perfectly straight parting: the hair of a film star. They didn't exchange any words. My mother cleaned the captain's wounds, changed his bandages, in silence. Rajesh Mudgal endured it all. He clenched his jaw, thinking of the sea: salty rain, waves as grey as elephants.

Slowly, very slowly, the patient improved, recovered his strength. My mother could tell by his eyes: new tiny wrinkles in the skin around their corners, a brilliance in the black lakes of his irises. Rajesh Mudgal's eyes were smiling. One morning, she began to long for them. Suddenly it was there, the longing, and it was warm and quick as lightning, everywhere and nowhere at once. Never before had she woken with such clarity, as if the new day's sun had been poured directly into her soul. Her body was made of light; her fingertips tingled.

She wondered what Rajesh Mudgal might be feeling. My mother tried to read his face. She saw furrows. The longer she looked, the more lines, the more creases of pain, she discovered: in his forehead, around his mouth, between his eyebrows. She was overcome by compassion. My mother took his hand, the hand with the five stumps for fingers. Squeezing it softly, she seemed to feel a spark. Startled, she dropped the hand. Suddenly, the situation dawned on her. She was a nurse; he was the scion of a wealthy family. He was an invalid; she was a woman in the prime of her life.

'We love but once, for once only are we perfectly equipped for loving,' Cyril Connolly writes in his memoir *The Unquiet Grave*. 'We may appear to ourselves to be as much in love at other times — so will a day in early September, though it be six hours shorter, seem as hot as one in June.' And he adds, like a dagger thrust: 'And on how that first true love affair will shape depends the pattern of our lives.'

Three years separated her farewell to Rajesh Mudgal and her meeting with Theodorus Henricus van der Kwast — three years in which my mother lived in various places and looked after other patients, cleaning their wounds, listening to their woes, and caressing their brows, but she never forgot Rajesh Mudgal's smiling eyes. They wrote each other long letters, with words that got more and more impressive. When my mother touched Rajesh Mudgal's words, she could feel the warmth in her body — the warmth that was everywhere and nowhere at once.

'It's better this way,' she told herself after saying goodbye to the captain. But she cried. And in the quiet house, her tears were as loud as a waterfall up in the mountains. The captain heaved himself out of bed and dragged his body across the floor to my mother. Not at sea, looking death in the eye, nor in hospital, waking up without his left foot, had the captain ever cried. But now the tears rolled down his cheeks, dripping onto the white tiles of the large, bright home.

The judge's voice remains etched on my mother's memory: 'Disappear and don't ever come back!' And so she went; she left without looking back, with her eyes cast down, fixed on the dust on the roads.

By the time my father falls in love with my mother, much of the pattern has been woven: dark thread, a shroud. They meet in the library of the Erasmus University in Rotterdam, where my father has a part-time job as a library assistant and my mother tries to come to grips with the angular Dutch language. She'd packed two suitcases, boarded a plane, and got off at Schiphol. Through a sister living in The Hague, she found a job as a nurse in Rotterdam. My mother wanted to get some experience abroad, but less than six months later she was ready to return. The words in the captain's letters were so big that my mother succumbed to them. But then she's offered a job as a theatre nurse. The hospital will pay for her training and give her a contract. She writes to the captain to say that she'll stay one more year before coming back with enough money for a house, in which she will look after him forever. There are no bigger words in a human life.

It's the last letter.

This is what happened: my father proposes marriage to my mother in the library. She says no right away. But my father doesn't understand her. He doesn't get the word *no*. The meaning of the word is suddenly beyond him. My mother repeats it.

'No,' she says. 'No, no, no.'

My father doesn't take no for an answer. He remains on his knees, waiting for the word we all wait for at least once in our lives.

In the days that follow, my mother says 'no' more than a million times. That, at any rate, is what has been passed down — passed down by *her*: 'I said *no* so many times that if I had a grain of rice for every no, it would feed the whole of India.'

This is followed by the tears, the tears that soften my mother, the tears to which I owe my existence. 'I felt sorry for him,' my mother tells me when, years after my birth, I ask her why in God's name she married my father. 'I couldn't bear any more pity, or shed any more tears.'

They got married one day early in September — warm, yet so much shorter than the endless days of longing in the hills of Agra. Those never-ending summer days. Three months later, my mother is pregnant. Gently, she caresses her belly, her fingertips tingling. And her body grows light again, even though it's the darkest month of the year: a rainy December.

The letters keep coming. The envelopes get thicker, the captain's words sadder. My mother doesn't have the heart to write him back.

My eldest brother is born at Dijkzigt Hospital in Rotterdam on 28 August 1977, at a quarter past seven in the morning. The baby's gender comes as a big surprise to my parents. They were expecting a girl; both had this strong gut feeling. It was probably the only feeling they ever shared, and perhaps wrong for that very reason. Their first child is a boy, and that boy now needs a name. My mother, her hair wet, her forehead still sweaty, comes up with Ashirwad. It's Indian for *gift from God*, just like Theodore. My father doesn't come up with anything. Perhaps he still can't believe he's holding a son in his arms: a small creature with pink arms, legs, and a willy.

Ashirwad van der Kwast. He's the firstborn, the eldest son, the pride and joy. Before the clock strikes noon, my mother makes her way to the bank located inside the hospital. In her arms she holds my brother — a shrivelled little pear, a groaning potato. His eyes are open, his dark eyes with that bluish tinge only newborns have. 'That swimming, sloping, elusive something', as Nabokov describes the baby iris blue, 'which seemed still to retain the shadows it had absorbed of ancient, fabulous forests where there were more birds than tigers and more fruit than thorns, and where, in some dappled depth, man's mind had been born.'

At the hospital branch of AMRO bank, my mother opens an account for my brother and deposits 1,000 guilders. My imagination deserts me when I try to picture where she gets those 1,000 guilders. Where were those bank notes during the delivery? In her hair? Under the bed? My mother hands the bank clerk the money, the money she saved up as a nurse, and thinks of the future, when Ashirwad is studying and dating girls and he can buy them drinks with her money. My brother sees ancient, fabulous forests, birds, and fruit, and groans softly — peaceful music on a peaceful day.

Their happiness is immense. It's the kind of happiness that only a firstborn generates: love so pure you can't imagine ever feeling it again. I think of the moments of light right after the birth of my son, my own firstborn — light so bright it illuminates everything: the days, the years, right up until this moment. And so I can visualise the happiness of 1977: a new life, a new dawn. Slowly, tender-loving-slowly, the little hands, the little fingers move. Slowly, the eyes open. And tender-loving-slowly, you can see the mind thinking, feeling, and wanting. My baby brother drinks from the breast, looks at everything shiny and reflective, and cries when it all becomes too much: the people, the things, the world. His eyes fall shut.

Then the days fly past. He touches everything and stuffs clothespegs and pencils into his mouth. His hands are grasping and groping, his legs trying hard to stand. My father leans over him, his hands under the boy's armpits, and so they make the first few steps together. Crowing — a smile trying to be bigger than the mouth that forms it.

If only time could issue a warning: gears that start grinding, a dial that starts slowing down. But no, time stands still, all of a sudden, just like that, and the clock never ticks again. My eldest brother has an epileptic seizure. With his arms and legs flailing and his eyes rolling, he stops breathing. It happens at night, in The Hague, where my mother is staying with her sister. Sleeping in the carrycot is Johan, my middle brother, two weeks old, his irises pale blue. Next to my mother, on the guest bed, is Ashirwad. She tries to insert a teaspoon between his tongue and his teeth. When I think of loneliness, I picture this desperate scene: my mother, my thrashing brother, and a teaspoon being wrenched into his mouth. My father is in Rotterdam, working on his PhD thesis — a study into mice with the red blood cells of sheep injected into them.

Twelve hours earlier, my parents had gone for a walk, pushing the dark-blue pram in which Johan was sighing and sleeping. I wasn't there; I hadn't been born yet. I've never looked up the weather report for Thursday 15 March 1979, and yet I can smell the air that day: paving slabs drying in the sun, crocuses, wet grass. The words evoke a dazzling day in spring, in the way that people with synaesthesia can see colours at the mention of numbers.

Ashirwad is with the next-door neighbour, the woman who will be known to me as Aunt Ank years later. She has offered to look after him, so my parents can go for a quiet stroll with the baby. At first my mother doesn't want to leave the house without Ashirwad, but my father manages to persuade her. She takes the boy to the neighbours, where she plants a kiss on his forehead, telling him they won't be far, they'll be back soon. She'll never forgive herself. Half an hour later, my mother is handed back a sick Ashirwad. His poo is green and foul-smelling. He's running a fever.

A crying baby, a sick child, and a thesis that needs to be finished: my mother decides to go and stay with her sister in The Hague. There, in a small room, in the dark, my eldest brother has a seizure. There, the tears that from now on will be my mother's constant companion, anywhere and anytime, start flowing.

A child doesn't understand grief. His world lets grief trickle through like sand does water. I never understood my mother's tears. Life was beautiful to me — full of joy and energy. I spent my time playing, running, and yelling. I learnt to write my name, figured out how much three times seven is, and told my parents the time. But in all this, my mother saw the things that Ashirwad would never be able to do.

It would be many years, dozens of visits to the consultant's office, and just as many examinations in hospital before the doctors finally diagnosed my brother. Hell for any parent. 'Learning disabilities' was the label attached to Ashirwad. The label was supposed to lighten the load. Now, at last, my parents knew what was wrong with their son; now they could carry on with their lives. But for my mother, time had frozen.

The older you get, the more grief you retain. It begins to cling to you, and you learn to take it all in. Yet I didn't understand my mother's grief until I was 27, until the summer I became a father myself. As I read *Job* by Joseph Roth, tears rolled down my cheeks.

The novel's subtitle is *the story of a simple man*. Its protagonist, Mendel Singer, a teacher at the village school and father to four children, is indeed a simple, God-fearing man: 'Hundreds of thousands before him had lived and taught as he did.' Yet his wife, Deborah, is one of a kind. She's the saddest of all mothers in literature. She was the one who first revealed to me the extent of my mother's grief. Deborah's son has a skull the size of a pumpkin, his legs are crooked and limp, and, like Ashirwad, he suffers epileptic seizures.

That grief is as big as an ocean — an infinite mass, deep and dark. Since her son Menuchim's birth, night has reigned supreme in Deborah's heart. Grief slinks into every joy; all celebrations are torture. And for Menuchim's mother, too, time stands still: 'There was no spring and no summer. All seasons were winter. The sun rose, but it did not warm. Hope alone refused to die.'

My mother's hope refused to die, too: the hope for a miracle. Year on year, the money in Ashirwad's savings account grows. Before bed, my mother tells me that in the future my eldest brother will take me everywhere in a car. She whispers to me, sitting at the foot of the bed. When I am a teenager and go to parties, Ashirwad will lend me a white shirt and give me pocket money. That's how it's done in Indian families; that's what an eldest son is for — the family's pride and joy. Then the light is switched off and my mother's footsteps die away in the night. The fairytales of my childhood were not *Sleeping Beauty* or *Cinderella*, but Ashirwad. He would become a doctor, buy a car, marry a beautiful princess, and live happily ever after.

Every morning, my mother combs a parting into Ashirwad's hair. Right now, he's still going to a school for children with severe learning disabilities, but as soon as her prayers are heard, he'll be going to primary school *de watertoren*, just like Johan and me. Mr De Gier, the head teacher, has already met him. My mother introduced him as follows: 'This is Ashirwad; he'll be skipping five classes soon.'

Day in, day out, Menuchim's mother prays to her Jewish God, but when her prayers aren't heard, she turns to her dead ancestors. She invokes her parents; Menuchim's grandfather, after whom her cripple son has been named; Abraham, Isaac, and Jakob; and Moses's bones. My mother, on her part, makes grateful use of the many Hindu gods.

First she addresses her prayers to Shiva, who's responsible for the destruction of evil. My mother sees Ashirwad's mental disability as an evil spirit that must be exorcised. This may sound harsh, but it isn't. (At a later stage, my mother will also pray to Shiva on Johan's and my behalf. My middle brother ends up marrying a Muslim woman, while I stop studying to start work on a novel. We, too, are possessed by an evil spirit that must be exorcised.) It's routine, good practice.

Praying is something my mother always does in the attic, a room we children are forbidden from entering. That said, every now and then we're allowed in on our stockinged feet. I remember my mother with a red, transparent shawl over her head, chanting softy and rocking back and forth. Incense fills the attic room with exotic fragrances and swirling coils of smoke that I try to follow. Here, too, are tears. But the tears rolling down my mother's cheeks in the prayer room dry faster than they do elsewhere. They seem to revitalise her. They're a shower of solace.

My mother tasks me with measuring the effects of her prayers to Shiva. And so, every day, I point to the antique wall clock in the living room and ask Ashirwad to tell me the time.

'Time to eat,' he usually says.

Or else: 'Time to watch television.'

Before long, my mother begins to address her prayers to Durga, the many-armed goddess who's often depicted seated on a tiger; Durga, the renowned slayer of demons. But Ashirwad remains Ashirwad. Even Krishna, the source of everything, is invoked, kneeling, singing, crying, and rocking. Many Hindu gods follow — a total of 52, the number to which my mother adheres. Some Hindus go with one or three; others swear by 30 million gods. My mother sticks to a reasonable 52, and when all of these gods have been invoked in vain, she concludes: 'You don't need to be able to tell the time to get your driver's licence.'

Hope springs eternal.

Yet something changes. My mother grows restless, irritable, and one day suspicion sneaks into her life. It's a form of paranoia that grows progressively stronger and comes to shape the rest of her life. The first time we're confronted with it, the whole family is sitting at the dinner table. We're eating spaghetti with ready-made tomato sauce when suddenly my mother shouts out: 'Kelly!' Nobody knows what's going on, or to whom my mother's referring. My father is the first to react. He chews and swallows his mouthful before asking: 'Veena, who's Kelly?'

Her eyes fill with tears: a sea to the left, a sea to the right. We don't breathe a word and look down at our plates.

'He ate Kelly's food,' my mother says, pointing to Ashirwad. 'When we took Johan for a walk in the pram and left Ashirwad with the neighbours, he ate dog food.'

Kelly is the neighbours' dog, Aunt Ank's Jack Russell. He's the new evil spirit.

My mother takes a deep breath. I can see the deluge welling up in her eyes. Her voice trembles when she speaks, when she says it was the dog food that caused Ashirwad's epileptic seizure.

Ashirwad is the only one who carries on eating, slurping up long strands of spaghetti.

And then my mother's eyes burst their banks. 'I didn't want to,' she screams. 'I didn't want to go out walking without Ashirwad. You forced me!' She takes off one of her slippers and hurls it in my father's direction. He manages to duck just in time. It's the first flying object in a long series punctuating my childhood. The second slipper does hit its target.

A plate follows, and then a glass, resulting in crashing shards, and tears streaming down her face like rivers.

Ashirwad puts down his cutlery and says: 'I don't like dog food.' He pulls a disgusted face, before picking up his cutlery again and taking a large mouthful of spaghetti with tomato sauce, his favourite food.

'Mum, are we eating snakies tonight?' he asks practically every day. To him, spaghetti is known as snakies; the pasta reminds him of snakes. He's got a point.

In the days that follow, Kelly has to fear for her life. My mother launches a guerrilla war against the neighbours' dark-brown-spotted Jack Russell. She chases the dog with her rolling pin and feeds the animal dog biscuits rubbed with hot chilli peppers, and when Kelly takes a piss outside our front door, my mother drops a telephone directory from the third floor. As sacred as the cow is to Indians, so devilish Kelly is to my mother.

The day after Aunt Ank's children complain about singed fur following a failed attempt to sacrifice the Jack Russell, the police turn up on our doorstep. My mother manages to give the officers the brush-off with a story about sparks jumping from the tandoori clay oven onto the dog. We don't actually own a tandoori clay oven, but why tell the officers that? They eat heartily from the chicken legs my mother dishes up, and even take some home to their wives. My mother's tandoori chicken is mouth-watering, and beyond compare in the Netherlands. How she does it without a traditional clay oven remains a mystery to me, but whoever has a taste of it is sold.

In the end, Kelly meets her demise by accident. She's run over by a garbage truck. It's the destructive force of chance — of fate, you might say — but my mother's adamant that Shiva is behind the fatal accident. At long last, the slayer of evil has done his job.

'If it hadn't been for Kelly, Ashirwad would be normal. Now that Kelly's gone, Ashirwad will be normal again.' These are my mother's words; this is her firm belief. And we gradually turn away from her — my father, my middle brother, and me. The only one who can't stand up to her is Ashirwad. He'll always be a four-year-old child, tied to his mother's apron strings. He takes her at her word.

'Ashirwad, one day you'll be better and you'll be able to tie your own shoelaces.'

'One day you'll be studying at Cambridge and become an eminent lawyer.'

'And when I'm old, Ashirwad, when your mother is grey and she spends all day in bed, you'll make me proud. You'll drop by in your chauffeured car and I'll kiss your forehead.'

There's a mine inside her, a shaft leading to an infinite store of hope. It's so dark down there you can't see a thing except darkness. But my mother finds solace in these subterranean vaults. Wandering through its tunnels, she's as lonely as she was the night Ashirwad suffered his epileptic seizure. She calls out his name, and the dark tunnels respond in a thousand voices. One day she'll recover him — her pride, her everything.

In *Job*, Deborah's eternal hope is nourished by the words of a holy man. When Menuchim is thirteen months old and he starts groaning like an animal, the desperate Deborah travels to the Rabbi of Kluczýsk. She's determined to gaze into the rabbi's eyes to see if they truly reflect the Almighty God. But her own eyes are oceans, and she sees the holy man from behind white waves of water and salt. And although he whispers, she hears his voice from up close: 'Menuchim, Mendel's son, will be healed. There will not be many like him in Israel … Have no fear, and go home!'

And so my mother and Deborah go on, while the bellows of hope keep moaning and groaning. Then, one day, the longed-for miracle happens. Menuchim utters his first word: 'Mama.'

Deborah's eyes fill with tears, sweet and warm this time.

'Mama,' Menuchim says again, and again, and a thousand times over.

Her son speaks. Her prayers haven't been in vain. 'It meant that Menuchim would be strong and big, wise and good, as the words of the blessing had promised.'

Wise and good: it sounds like the profile of a judge, or a lawyer. Menuchim, too, is headed for a glorious career. Besides 'mummy', my eldest brother could also say, 'Daddy, why do you always shake your head?' But he can't read or write. He still can't by the time he's twelve, and my mother continues to comb his hair into a side parting. Every morning, she sprinkles Ashirwad's thick, dark hair with a watering can in the garden, before combing it into a perfectly straight parting. 'How handsome you are,' I often hear her mutter. 'The girls will be all over you.'

One glorious morning in summer, the comb drops from my mother's hands. 'Rajesh Mudgal,' she says, the way she once uttered Kelly's name. It's the sun sparkling on my brother's black hair, on the parting — the hair of a film star. My mother screams the captain's name, and again, a thousand times over.

From that day on, Rajesh Mudgal is back in my mother's life, and a new feature of ours. We're sitting at the table, eating spaghetti with tomato sauce, as my mother unfolds her theory. We keep calm and carry on eating, my father and my brothers. We've heard worse. This is the theory: Ashirwad is disabled because of a curse put on him by the captain. My mother tells us about Rajesh Mudgal. Like Ashirwad, he was the firstborn, the eldest son, the family's pride and joy. 'He had two toes, half a right hand, and no left foot. But he had eyes that smiled like spring and summer.' Not much later, the first slipper comes flying at my father, followed by several other items on the table. My mother yells that it's all his fault. If he hadn't proposed marriage to her, she'd have married the captain. And if she'd married the captain, Ashirwad wouldn't be here now.

This is what she yells; this is what she cries.

Like Mendel Singer, my father is a simple man. He picks up the slippers and carries them back to my mother. He gathers up the shards of glass and the bits of food.

Ashirwad puts his cutlery down for a moment. 'It's a good thing Mummy didn't marry the captain.' Then he carries on shovelling food into his mouth.

'Days drew themselves out into weeks, weeks grew into months, twelve months made a year.' And ten years turns my mother into a woman possessed — possessed by hope. She takes Ashirwad to mass healings with Jomanda in Tiel, a famous medium, and she takes him to Lourdes. Anything that reeks of miracles is given a go. Wizards, clairvoyants, and spiritualists — they're all on the list. There's even a visit to a psychic fakir in a Rotterdam suburb. By then, Ashirwad is 22, averse to physical contact and prone to temper tantrums. When the fakir tries to pierce my eldest brother's cheek with a needle, the man has to pay for it with a black eye. Even next-door neighbours, postmen and -women, and bus drivers are no longer safe. And sometimes my mother gets hit, too. Ashirwad is 1.96 metres, my mother more than a foot shorter. When he flies into a rage, there's nothing she can do except shout, telling him to stop kicking and lashing out. And when he's finally calm again, she tells him: 'I love you so much, Ashirwad. You're my darling, my firstborn, my pride and joy.' Confused and crying his eyes out, he puts his head on my mother's shoulder. She's crying too, and always confused, and rests her head on his.

Once upon a time she was a white apparition in the sun, with the crisp aura of youth, beauty, and innocence.

If only she'd never left.

If only she'd never married my father.

If only she'd never gone for a walk without Ashirwad.

This is what she tells herself. This is what she'll never stop telling herself. And she caresses Ashirwad's dark hair.

By then, I've already left home. Likewise, my middle brother is living somewhere else, in Utrecht, where he's studying physical geography. We only come home at the weekends, with our dirty laundry and empty stomachs.

Sometimes we eat tandoori chicken, but usually snakies.

❁

Then comes the moment Ashirwad leaves home, too. He moves into an assisted living facility for disabled people on Corrie Hartonglaan, a ten-minute bike ride from Tiberiaslaan, where my parents now live. Although it's the best solution all around, my mother is struggling to come to terms with it. Every day she cycles over to see her eternal four-year-old. She asks him what he did in daycare, how much he's eaten, what shows he's seen on television. And then she cycles home again, where it's quiet and she's afraid she might hear her own tears drop.

On Corrie Hartonglaan, Ashirwad lives with seven other people — or clients, as they're called. There's Jopie, who likes to plunge her hands into a bowl of sweetcorn; Rik, who's crazy about Michael Jackson; and Arno, who's always dressed in his football kit: Feyenoord shirt, Feyenoord pants, and Feyenoord scarf (even in summer). One of them teaches Ashirwad the word *handicapped*. But he doesn't agree with the meaning; that's to say, he doesn't think it applies to him. One day, when my mother is visiting, Ashirwad says: 'I'm not handicapped. I'm Ashirwad.'

My mother nods and says: 'You're a gift, a gift from God.'

Like many other Jews, the Singer family emigrates to the United States, where they hope to secure a better future. Menuchim stays behind, even though the

Rabbi of Kluczýsk has entreated Deborah: 'Do not send him away from your side; he is yours even as a healthy child is.'

The hope, the unfailing, the undying hope, had finally crumbled and blown away. The miracle Menuchim's mother had been waiting for all those years — 'day and night, hour after hour' — hasn't come to pass.

My parents emigrate to Canada, and Ashirwad stays behind, too. My father sets off first, and months later my mother boards a plane as well — with all her earthly belongings, except her children. On the day of her departure, I was abroad myself, so I didn't get to say goodbye to her or see what the parting between she and Ashirwad was like. I only know how painful the other goodbye was: 'Weeping, she climbed into the wagon. She did not see the faces of the people whose hands she pressed. Her two eyes were two great oceans of tears. She heard the clatter of the horses' hooves. She was off. She cried aloud; she did not know that she cried aloud; something cried in her; her heart had a mouth and cried.'

The grief that once flowed through me like water flows through sand, and that later began to stick to me like a wet leaf in autumn — that grief now suffocates me. It's the grief for children who'll never learn to read, write, do arithmetic, or tell time; who'll never go on dates, but who'll grow quieter and start pulling out their own eyebrows and lashes, because they don't understand themselves.

Ashirwad never skipped five classes. He never skipped a single class.

In the end, Menuchim does quite well for himself, although his mother doesn't live to see this. Deborah dies before the great miracle manifests itself. Several months after her death, Mendel Singer meets his long-lost son in New York. He fails to recognise him. Menuchim is a handsome young man in evening wear. Going by the name of Alexis Kossak, he's now a world-famous composer.

Granted, that's not quite up there with a doctor or a lawyer.

And now that the ocean divides us and we've all gone our separate ways, we communicate on Skype: a crackling connection, a picture that's blurred and keeps jumping. Sometimes I can't hear my mother, or else there's a delay, so we're constantly talking over each other. But it's free. And anything that's free is good. So say Indians; so says my mother.

When I tell her I'm writing a story about Ashirwad, she nods. It's early morning in Toronto; it's still dark. Since my mother saves energy by not making use of lamps, her face is illuminated only by the screen: a white square on a dark, deeply creased face.

'All right,' she says. And after a long while, which may be shorter than it feels: 'You can write what you want, invent and distort everything. Everything. Just don't say I ever gave up hope.'

The screen freezes. My mother has turned to stone. The speakers emit a waterfall of noise.

I don't know if she can see me or hear me.

I promise.

FREE IS GOOD

The journey started in Rotterdam, on Oudedijk, the Mecklenburglaan stop. Ashirwad kept looking to the left, waiting for the yellow number seven tram to appear in the distance. Around his neck he wore a rectangular travel purse. It held no notes, no coins with which to buy French fries or ice-cream. The purse was empty, save for one item: a pass with his name, date of birth, photo, and the following description: 'Disabled person's companion pass.' This pass allowed whoever accompanied Ashirwad to travel on public transport for free, be it tram, bus, or train. My mother had applied to the city council for it, and the day the pass landed on our doorstep, our lives became even more circumscribed. From then on, we'd have to travel with Ashirwad if we were taking public transport, so one of us would be travelling for free. Free is good.

Sometimes (when Ashirwad was in school, or in bed with the flu), the pass alone sufficed. On those occasions, I'd wear the travel purse around my neck and look around in surprise when the ticket inspector turned up: 'Ashirwad? Ashirwad, where are you?' The conductor always allowed me to get off immediately to search for my brother.

The other scenario was that I'd be joined by my middle brother Johan (who, aside from asthma, is perfectly healthy). Whenever we had our tickets checked, I'd show the pass and Johan would pull a funny face. 'He's disabled,' I'd often say, perhaps unnecessarily, to the conductor, who'd nod his understanding.

'Nine,' Ashirwad shouted. 'Tram number nine.' To the left, in the distance, a yellow vehicle appeared. My mother peered at the approaching tram, but her eyes weren't good enough to distinguish between a seven and a nine. It wasn't until the tram reached the stop that she said: 'Well done, Ashirwad.' And she let go of the handles of her suitcases.

It goes without saying that the journey had commenced earlier — at home, in my mother's wardrobes. Whenever my mother travelled, she tried to transfer the contents of these wardrobes to the suitcases — or as much as possible, anyway. For example, when we went on holiday to the United States, we racked up a total of seventeen suitcases; fourteen for our midweek break to amusement park De Efteling. All I remember about some holidays is the number of suitcases.

That morning, the contents of the wardrobes had been transferred to four large cases. They were bursting with clothes, pots and pans, food, and items that might be of use while in transit. Those who had to buy something while travelling hadn't really got the hang of life, weren't really up to the challenge — if my mother was to be believed, anyway.

Suitcases, always these suitcases.

My father lugged them to the tram stop on Oudedijk. He'd become an accomplished porter and wouldn't look out of place at Mumbai Central station. Perhaps he was even better than the average porter — nimbler and faster.

Ashirwad gave the driver of tram nine the finger. He did that sort of thing since he'd hit puberty. If something wasn't to his liking, he could flip.

When the tram drove off with a chime, my mother walked over to Ashirwad. 'You mustn't show your middle finger,' she said. 'Don't you know what it means?'

'I want tram seven to come.'

'It'll be here in a minute.'

'Mummy,' my brother said. 'Where are we going?'

'We're going on a long journey,' my mother replied. 'We're going to France.'

'With line seven?'

'First we'll take line seven, then the train, and then a coach.'

'Where am I sleeping tonight?'

'In a hotel.'

'And how about Teddy?' My brother had a soft toy, a stuffed monkey he called Teddy. He slept with it under his armpit. Since Ashirwad hit puberty, Teddy smelled like the changing room of a rugby club.

'Teddy's in the suitcase,' my mother said.

'So he's also taking the tram, the train, and the coach?'

My mother nodded. Ashirwad had no more questions — either about the journey or about France. He felt reassured. He looked to the left again, eager for tram number seven to appear. That was my brother all over. One moment he'd lay into someone, the next he was worried about his cuddly toy.

At Rotterdam Central station, my mother accosted a police officer. She pointed to the four suitcases next to her on the ground, and then at Ashirwad, just like I'd point to Johan when we had our tickets inspected on the tram or bus. With this difference: my mother didn't say 'He's disabled,' and Ashirwad didn't pull a funny face. The disabled person's companion pass had to suffice. My mother pulled the pass from my brother's travel purse and showed it to the officer. 'We need to get to Platform 11,' she said. That's where the train to Utrecht was due to depart from in three minutes' time. My father would pull it off easily — four suitcases, three minutes, eleven platforms — but he'd been sent back home from the Oudedijk tram stop without a tip. He couldn't travel for free. And not free was not good.

Now the police officer was expected to carry the cases. He read the text on the pass carefully, unsure what was expected of him. So my mother said: 'Come on, Ashirwad, let's get a move on.'

The police officer arrived at the train ten minutes late. My mother was standing in the doorway, having a heated discussion with the train manager. She was making a terrible fuss, shouting that the police were on their way, that she was being escorted by the police. There are times when I'm absolutely thrilled to be elsewhere. The police officer was sweating like a pig; his blue shirt was drenched, his cap askew on his head. He wouldn't stand a chance at Mumbai Central station, but this was Rotterdam Central station; the two were a world apart. My mother opened one of the suitcases and began to rummage around in it. Finally, she felt what she was looking for, and from among the various odds and ends extracted a tin of cat food. It was mashed rabbit, bought on special, one of the last few tins. The whistle drowned out the police officer's cries of surprise.

The train journey went well; that's to say, without any tantrums. My brother looked out of the window, hummed songs he'd heard on the radio, and proudly pulled the companion pass out of his purse when the conductor entered the compartment. As the man inspected the pass, Ashirwad pointed to my mother and said: 'She's disabled,' a joke my brother and me had taught him.

At Utrecht station, they were met by a nephew who helped them with the luggage. He was the son of one of my mother's sisters and lived downtown. The previous day my mother had phoned my aunt in The Hague, demanding that her son come and collect her from the station. The conversation was in Hindi; the only Dutch words were *Jaarbeurs Utrecht*, repeated over and over. This was where my mother and brother would be boarding a coach. The nephew entered the exhibition centre car park and stopped beside the first touring coach he spotted. But this wasn't the one that would take my mother and brother to France. A notice behind the windscreen said *Cologne*. My mother ordered the nephew to go ask the driver. Reluctantly, he got out and made his way to the coach. A moment later, he got back into the car and started the engine. 'We need to be a bit further up, to the right,' the nephew said. Several coaches were parked over there, so what followed was an interminable search. The nephew drove up to coach after coach, only to be told over and over again that my mother and brother weren't on the passenger list. He didn't give up; he couldn't give up. A nephew has a duty to his aunt — this is how things are done in Indian culture. By now, my mother was seething and told her nephew off for failing to locate the coach. This is not how things are done in Indian culture; this is just how my mother does things. She swore at him and yanked at the steering wheel when she thought he was going the wrong way. Sometimes other people would be equally thrilled to be elsewhere.

At long last, the right coach was located, but my mother wasn't on the passenger list. Ashirwad was.

'What about Teddy?' my brother asked the driver.

The driver scrolled down the list with his index finger. 'Ted,' he said. 'And the last name is …?'

People often take Ashirwad seriously, because he looks perfectly normal: a handsome young man with a parting in his hair. It was impossible to tell, just from looking at him, that he couldn't read or write. The only progress he'd made in all those years was that he could now tell tram seven from tram nine.

My mother stepped between the driver and my brother. 'Teddy's in the suitcase,' she said. 'He travels in the luggage compartment.'

'People aren't allowed to travel in the luggage compartment,' the driver said.

'Teddy's not a person. Teddy's a monkey.'

Confusion all around, but trust my mother to make things even worse. She pulled the companion pass out of the travel purse and handed it to the driver, telling him with a smile: 'I travel for free.'

The driver looked at the pass, the way the police officer had done earlier, the way countless innocent people had done at one time or another: cashiers, swimming pool attendants, shoe sellers. My mother could have been a sister of Dimitri Verhulst's mother. There's a story in the Flemish author's novel *The Misfortunates* about Mother Verhulst's 'pee pass': 'At a theatre or cinema box office she would fish all kinds of cards up out of her handbag and the pee pass trumped the lot. It stopped people in their tracks and they would often give her a discount to put an end to her moaning.' My mother, too, would produce her pass wherever she went. If it didn't give her free travel, she demanded a reduction: in entrance fees to museums and swimming pools, in prices in shops.

'This pass is for use on public transport only,' the driver said, and returned it to my mother. Two non-insulated wire ends in my mother's head made contact. Her smile vanished instantly. 'It doesn't say so,' she replied, and quickly slipped the pass back into the travel purse. 'In India, I even get to fly for free with this pass,' she said proudly.

When the driver refused to budge, my mother decided to change tack. She placed one foot on the bus and declared in a loud voice: 'I get to accompany my son for free because he's mentally handicapped.' My mother never normally said this in Ashirwad's presence, but the short-circuit in her head overrode this rule. She was determined to travel to France for free. And she knew Ashirwad would get angry, furious, livid. He didn't like people calling him handicapped.

Not long ago, he'd started throwing shoes about in a shop when my mother explained to the salesman why she had a right to a discount.

Ashirwad raised both middle fingers to the driver and shouted: 'Lesbian dickhead!'

Dickhead was my brother's favourite insult. Some days we were all dickheads at home: my parents, my brother, me, the guinea pig. The addition of 'lesbian' was a new thing. Ashirwad must have learned it from some of the local children. The woman at Number Nine was a lesbian. Although my brother didn't have a clue what the word actually meant, that didn't stop him from using it.

'Do you want to take him on his own?' my mother asked the driver, and placed her other foot inside the bus, too.

Not much later, the driver hoisted four large suitcases into the luggage compartment, moaning all the while. (The nephew had already been sent home without a tip.) Nobody could stand up to my mother. In a different life she might have been a dictator, a despot who'd make the history books. In this one, she was my Indian mother, and Ashirwad's, too.

Unlike the train journey, the coach trip didn't go off quite so smoothly. In front of, behind, and next to Ashirwad sat people who were wearing white caps and singing songs. Ashirwad only liked one type of song:

the hits on Radio 538. The commercial station was always on in my father's car. Other stations and other songs weren't conducive to his good mood, and even less so to that of the people around him. The songs the people on the bus were singing were cheerful and all about God: *'Do you know your Father knows you? / Do you know he cares? / Do you know you're a treasure / A treasure in God's hand?'*

My brother stuck his fingers in his ears and began to sing the latest big 538 hit: Fatboy Slim's 'Fucking in Heaven'. Who Fatboy Slim was or what 'fucking' meant — or 'fucking in heaven' for that matter — was all a mystery to Ashirwad. But the people around him took him seriously because he looked normal. They tried to drown him out with: *'Clap your hands, for the Lord is good / Stamp your feet, for the Lord is good.'* Ashirwad pressed his fingers deeper into his ears and roared the words 'fucking in heaven' over the clapping and stamping.

And then my mother, who'd been snoring all this time, woke up. She has the great gift of instantly falling asleep in all moving vehicles. And deny it though she will, she snores like a chainsaw. Confused and alarmed by the din around her, she asked: 'What's going on?' But Ashirwad had his fingers in his ears and kept shouting. The woman in the seat in front of my mother turned around to say that the young man next to her was singing Satanic songs.

'Ashirwad,' my mother said. 'Stop it, please stop

shouting.' She grabbed hold of his trembling hands and caressed his forehead while whispering in his ear: 'You're my darling, my firstborn, my pride and joy. I love you so much.' And when he was finally calm and quiet again, my mother took the companion pass out of the travel purse and handed it to the woman in front of her.

'Could you hand this around?' my mother asked her.

And so the document was passed around the coach, from hand to hand, from front to back. People read the text, looked at the photo, and nodded to my mother to convey their understanding. It turned out that the pass served to broker peace, too.

At the rest stop, one of the passengers gave Ashirwad a white cap. *God is Good*, it said on the visor. 'And free, too,' my mother added, but that was lost on everyone.

The rest of the journey passed quietly. There was no more singing; instead, everybody watched a film shown on two small television sets. Unlike radio, my brother liked all television. It didn't matter what was being broadcast: wildlife documentaries, sport, soap operas — anything was interesting. That said, things didn't get truly exciting unless there was kissing involved, or *Baywatch* was on. In that case, Ashirwad would giggle loudly, and every time a breast appeared on screen, he'd say: 'Whoa there!' The film on the coach gave little cause for giggling. It was the story of

Jesus, from cradle to grave. My mother was asleep, her eyes closed. Every couple of minutes, Ashirwad woke her up, because her snoring bothered him.

'You're snoring through the film,' he kept saying.

'No, I'm not,' my mother replied, getting angrier by the minute. She even began to swear in Hindi. Unlike Fatboy Slim's English profanities, Ashirwad knew perfectly well what these expletives meant. The fruits of one's mother tongue …

At some point, other people began to take offence at the snoring, too. Having woken my mother for the umpteenth time, only to hear her deny the snoring again, my brother received the backing of a fellow passenger.

'I can hear it, too,' the man behind her said. 'You're snoring very loudly.'

'No, I'm not,' my mother replied. 'I'm not snoring at all.'

'Like a chainsaw,' someone else chipped in.

My mother shook her head angrily, before erupting in a barrage of Indian swearwords that continued for at least five kilometres. The entire coach looked over, a sea of *God is Good* caps.

My mother really ought to have her own pass, featuring her name, date of birth, photo, and the following warning: 'Run if you want a happy life.'

Just before they arrived in Lourdes, one of the passengers walked to the front and began to address the coach through a microphone. She made a few announcements of a practical nature: rubbish in the bin, applause for the driver, which groups were sleeping where, and what time dinner was served. She concluded with a prayer. Ashirwad asked my mother which group they belonged to. 'We belong together,' my mother said. What she meant was that she'd only booked the coach journey; once in Lourdes, they'd have to find their own accommodation.

It was the same story on family holidays — we always did it without any planning. The region in France, Germany, or Luxembourg would have been chosen, but we never booked a hotel or an apartment in advance. My mother had no faith in travel agencies. She preferred to do everything herself. I remember a holiday in Baden-Baden in Germany, when we spent the first four nights in the car, a red Lada 2000. All the holiday chalets were too expensive for my mother's liking.

'I'm a professor,' my father said after yet another chalet had been rejected. 'I earn enough to buy this house.'

'You don't even earn enough to buy a dog kennel,' my mother replied, and started the car. The faster we got out of this place, the better. Free was good; too expensive was evil.

'It's a great place for the children,' my father tried.

But my mother was unrelenting. And unreasonable, too. She converted the chalet prices from Deutschmark to Dutch guilders, and then from Dutch guilders to Indian rupees. Without adjusting for inflation, out of all proportion.

In the end, we found shelter in a shed rented out by an old lady. The place reeked of dung.

In Lourdes, my mother had a choice of 300 hotels. I have no idea how many receptionists, hotel owners, and bellboys my mother spoke to, and how many people were shown the companion pass. As my mother knows I'm writing a book about our family, she's stopped answering my questions, and to Ashirwad, eight is just as many as 80. But if you ask him if he'd like to go back to Lourdes, he'll shake his head furiously.

In the end, my mother opted for Hôtel les Rosiers, because the following week the washing line at her house boasted two yellow towels with the name of this hotel woven into them. The material was thick; the font, elegant. To my mother, the price of a hotel room is all-inclusive. That's to say, it's inclusive of breakfast, service, towels, linen, and everything on the wall. We once took a pair of antlers from a German guesthouse.

That evening, my mother and Ashirwad joined a candlelight procession. Thousands of people holding candles, on foot, in wheelchairs, or in beds on wheels, formed an iridescent parade that snaked along the

Esplanade du Rosaire, behind a large statue of the Virgin Mary. My mother had tears in her eyes and never let go of my brother's hand. She prayed the Rosary, even though she's a Hindu, and isn't familiar with either the Hail Mary or the Lord's Prayer. She just muttered along, the way Ashirwad mutters along to new songs on the radio — songs he hasn't heard before but still wants to sing.

In the hotel room, Ashirwad cuddled up to Teddy in bed. My mother tucked them in, and sang the Indian lullaby she used to sing for me and my brother Johan: '*Chandaa maama door ke, puye pakaayen boor ke. Aap khaayen thaali mein, munne ko den pyaali mein …*' Even though it was never on Radio 538, it was a song Ashirwad liked to hear. My mother had been singing it to him for 20 years now — an eternal lullaby.

In the other bed, my mother had trouble falling asleep because Ashirwad's snoring was possibly even louder than her own. But she didn't wake him up. My mother stared at the hotel room ceiling, at the spiderwebs, the stains and the cracks — the sinuous cracks that many before her had gazed at in the almost-dark while saying their prayers. She thought about her firstborn, her pride and joy; about a large car he would be driving in the future and a princess who would kiss him. Then, finally, she fell asleep.

The following morning at eight, breakfast was served. Each table had a basket with bread and various toppings. It didn't take my mother long to

see that there was one croissant, one roll, two small
tubs of jam, and a tiny packet of butter per person.
She complained even before she got to her seat. The
French lady who walked around with a coffee pot
fobbed her off by saying she didn't speak English. She
clearly hadn't counted on my mother's tenacity. While
Ashirwad devoured the rolls and all the toppings,
my mother snuck off to the kitchen. The coffee lady
couldn't believe her eyes. She'd seen many pilgrims
in her lifetime, but none of them had ever stolen
bread and tubs of jam from the kitchen. Not that it
was stealing to my mother. She never stole — she
had a right to these things, she'd paid for them. And
so, brazenly, she actually returned to the kitchen a
little later so she could prepare sandwiches for lunch.
Because let's face it: a half-decent hotel breakfast also
covers your midday meal.

On Thursday 11 February 1858, the Virgin Mary
appeared to Bernadette Soubirous in the Grotto of
Massabielle in Lourdes. Bernadette, fourteen years of
age and the daughter of a poor miller, was collecting
wood and bones with her sister and a friend. As the girl
was about to cross the stream in the grotto barefoot,
she spotted a lady: 'She was wearing a white gown as
well as a white veil, a blue girdle, and a yellow rose on
each foot.' Together they said the Lord's Prayer, and
then the Virgin Mary disappeared again.

Seventeen more visions followed. On one of those occasions, the stream turned into a well, and Bernadette drank the water: 'She told me to drink from the well.' Less than a week later, the first miracle occurred: after 38-year-old Catherine Latapie from Loubajac stuck her paralysed arm into the water of the well, she was able to move both her arm and hand again.

The Catholic Church confirmed the authenticity of the apparitions in 1862, and in 1873 the first pilgrimage took place. Since then, Lourdes has been visited by countless pilgrims from around the world — some five million a year these days. The water from the well is now thought to have brought about more than 60 miracles: restoring sight to the blind, curing cancer patients of their tumours, and giving the mentally ill their peace of mind again.

My mother visited the grotto with Ashirwad by the hand. Despite the early hour, there was already a long queue. They were mostly elderly, with groups of young people here and there. Somewhere halfway down the queue, my mother spotted a group wearing white caps on their heads. She briefly considered putting Ashirwad's *God is Good* cap on his head to jump the queue, but she had a better idea. There was a separate queue for the disabled. People on crutches, in wheelchairs, or in beds on wheels got in almost immediately.

'What are you doing?' my brother asked when my mother stepped out of the line of shuffling pensioners.

'*Chup ho djao*,' my mother said, which means 'be quiet' in Hindi. But more than that, it's a kind of secret agreement, a pact between her and Ashirwad. Whenever my mother spoke those three Indian words, or just a succinct '*Chup*', my brother knew she was up to something.

Five minutes later, my mother returned with a wheelchair. She told Ashirwad to sit down, but he shook his head.

'You want *tikkie*?' my mother asked and raised her hand.

Tikkie, or slap, was another one of those secrets words. I was familiar with it, too — and with the dire consequences if you didn't obey.

After some grumbling, my brother sat down in the wheelchair. The people in the queue watched it all in bemusement. Ashirwad had no mobility problems — in fact, he had no physical disabilities whatsoever. Several pilgrims shook their head; some reacted angrily. The miracle was supposed to make people get out of their wheelchairs, not have them end up in one. My mother took no notice of the protests and wheeled Ashirwad to the front, to the grotto where the Virgin Mary had appeared before Bernadette. My brother kept quiet. Maybe he was trying to avoid a scene, the way I'd spent my childhood trying to avoid scenes.

But while it may have been in my mother's nature to try and get one over on others, always and anywhere, she was also doing it for Ashirwad — first and foremost for Ashirwad. He'd waited long enough for a cure.

Inside the grotto, people touched the rock face with their fingers, or with their lips. Some pilgrims even rubbed photos against the wall — of a sick grandma, or of a baby in an incubator. Again, my mother's eyes filled with tears: waxing seas, tidal waves of sorrow. She pulled the companion pass out of the travel purse and pressed it against the grey rock. Softly, very softly, she said a prayer, chanting the words, as she did in the prayer room in the attic.

That's when Ashirwad got up. He'd become curious and wanted to touch the rockface, like the others. Suddenly, people began to applaud, and joyous cheers rang through the queue. A Japanese woman fainted. My mother got angry and gestured for Ashirwad to sit down again. While swearing in Hindi, she wheeled him out of the sacred grotto.

The wheelchair was returned to an Indian man sitting on the ground. My mother offered him lunch, consisting of a croissant and a small tub of jam.

Next up, my mother and brother visited the seventeen baths. Into these baths flowed the water from the well that Bernadette drank from, water that was said to have healing powers. It was the water for which my mother had come all the way from Rotterdam, for which pilgrims kept coming from all over the world.

If anything, Ashirwad thought the water was cold.

There was a Dutch nun beside one of the baths. She wore a white robe and introduced herself as Sister Johanna.

'Ashirwad,' my brother said. 'Number Three Tiberiaslaan, 3061 BJ, Rotterdam.' Since he'd learned his full address, including postcode, by heart, he told it to everyone to whom he introduced himself. Sometimes he even added his favourite food: 'Snakies.' But not this time.

'Mrs Van der Kwast,' my mother said. This is how she answered the phone; this is how she introduced herself. Her passport said Veena Ahluwalia, but we'd never heard that first and last name. It was an untold story, a mystery.

Sister Johanna accompanied pilgrims to the changing room and helped them in and out of the water. She was about to take Ashirwad by the hand when my mother stopped her.

'We belong together,' she said again, and walked with him to the changing room.

It was true. If there were two people in this world who belonged together, they were my mother and my eldest brother: the snoring twosome, the inseparable mother and son who had an implicit understanding. All children want to come along to the baker or the bank, but even though Ashirwad had long ceased to be a child, he still asked 'Can I come, too?' every time my mother left the house.

My mother was the first to enter the water. She dipped her head under for ten seconds. Those with enough faith in the water's healing powers would be cured, just like Catherine Latapie, Antonia Moulin, Vittorio Micheli, Leo Schwager, Cécile Douville de Franssu, and so on and so forth. The list of names kept growing. Anna Santaniello was the most recent one to be added to the inventory of miracles. In 1952, she paid a visit to the baths and was cured of severe rheumatoid arthritis. When the Church recognised the miracle half a century later, on 9 November 2005, Anna Santaniello became the 67th pilgrim to have been officially healed in Lourdes. It happened in the nick of time, because the old lady wasn't much longer for this world; only another three weeks and two days, to be precise.

Sister Johanna helped my mother out of the bath. My mother was shivering, and her lips were blue. Water dripped onto the tiles.

Then it was Ashirwad's turn. He dipped one foot into the bath. No sooner had he done so than he squealed.

'And now your right foot,' Sister Johanna said.

Ashirwad shook his head. 'Cold,' he just about managed to utter.

'It takes a bit of getting used to.'

This was followed by giggles. Ashirwad's eyes had wandered to an image on the wall of the bathing area: Maria holding Jesus in her arms, one of her breasts bared. 'Whoa there!' my brother exclaimed. 'Whoa there!'

My mother lowered her eyes. It was high time for a miracle.

Sister Johanna whispered a prayer, the way she'd done when my mother got into the bath. Ashirwad was still watching the icon, as though it were a television screen — *Baywatch* without sound.

'Your other foot,' my mother ordered.

The only thing Ashirwad moved was his head. He shook it.

My mother raised her hand. '*Tikkie*? You want *tikkie*?'

Moaning and groaning followed, but then my brother's right foot did disappear into the water.

'Well done,' the nun said.

Ashirwad just stood there in the bath, like a statue with chattering teeth. He didn't know where he was or what was happening to him; why his mother was looking at him with bated breath or why the woman in the white robe was whispering. And who can blame him? It *was* incomprehensible, even for someone capable of reading, writing, arithmetic, and telling time.

My mother folded her hands — she'd never been this close to a miracle before. Perhaps the son who'd been born to her, her gift, would finally be returned to her.

'You need to lie down,' the nun told him.

'Oh boy, oh boy!' Reluctantly, Ashirwad sat down in the bath, his knees sticking out of the water.

'Freezing cold,' he commented. Then he stretched out his left leg, followed by his right one, before slipping completely underwater — his face, chest, knees, and toes.

The most recent cure dates back to 1987, when the Frenchman Jean-Pierre Bély was cured of multiple sclerosis. Eleven years earlier, twelve-year-old Delizia Cirolli from Italy got out of her wheelchair, and would never need it again. 'Those with enough faith will be healed,' my mother's inner voice said. 'Those with enough faith …'

Suddenly Ashirwad leapt up. His eyes were closed, and goosebumps covered his arms and his belly. With the water gushing over his body, he gasped for breath.

Reborn, my mother thought. He's been reborn.

Then Ashirwad's eyes opened. The first person he saw was Sister Johanna in her white robe. 'Lesbian dickhead,' he yelled at the top of his lungs. 'Filthy lesbian dickhead!'

The nun quickly crossed herself. My mother tried to calm my brother by wrapping a towel around his shoulders. But Ashirwad wouldn't be calmed. 'Lesbian dickhead,' echoed through the bathing area again. Even his ears were covered in goosebumps.

The nun crossed herself again. Every time my brother yelled at her, she crossed herself. She'd never crossed herself so many times.

Ashirwad shivered with cold. Intent on revenge, he began to splash the water about with his hands and feet. The nun's robe got drenched.

'*Ashirwad!*'

My mother screamed his name with all her might. It drowned out the splashing and the swearing, the anger and the devotion. In an instant, all was quiet.

Ashirwad looked shamefaced as he glanced over at my mother. Her cheeks were wet. It was impossible to tell whether they were wet with tears or holy water.

That afternoon, the coach returned to Utrecht. There was just enough time to buy a souvenir, or to have an ice-cream at an outdoor café. But my mother had something else in mind. The bellboy of the Hôtel les Rosiers followed her with the four suitcases. They were on their way to the taps beside the grotto. Ashirwad asked: 'What are we doing?'

'Taking water home,' my mother replied.

Ashirwad nodded. He didn't ask any more questions; he felt reassured. The bellboy, however, didn't know what was about to hit him.

The arrival of a water meter in our house had imposed yet another limitation on our lives. The meter registered use; instead of a fixed sum, we now had to pay for every litre consumed. In other words: every little drop cost us money. My mother had managed to keep the water company's installation engineers at bay for months. When someone rang the doorbell, we weren't allowed to make a peep — as if the Gestapo was at the door. But one day our number was up, and the water meter was attached to our mains. From then on, there was no more wasting water — not even a droplet. We weren't allowed to shower for longer than one minute a week; the toilet flush mechanism was dismantled — we'd now flush by emptying a bucket of rainwater; there were pots under the taps to catch water that would otherwise be lost — water that would then be boiled for tea or used to do the dishes; all our plants were thrown out. And, last but not least, we smuggled water home: from school, from work, from the athletics club, from pretty much anywhere.

The bellboy put the four suitcases down on the ground. My mother opened them one after the other and took out six blue jerrycans. It was a magic trick. In the next town, she would conjure up a herd of sheep from these suitcases.

Other pilgrims bought Lourdes water in a bottle shaped like the Virgin Mary and took it home as a souvenir. My mother filled six large jerrycans: 180 litres of water. For the foreseeable future, our water meter wouldn't budge.

Again, pilgrims shook their heads; again, people voiced their disapproval. These were noises that surrounded my mother like a swarm of insects, that went wherever she went.

While the second jerrycan was filling up under the tap and the bellboy was biting his nails, my mother tried to neaten Ashirwad's hair. The bath had messed it all up. But my mother couldn't reach his head. Ashirwad was nearly six foot six; my mother over a foot shorter. Holding a comb in her left hand and water in her right, she clambered on top of one of her cases. And so she combed Ashirwad's hair into a parting, the neat, perfectly straight parting of a film star and the captain buried deep in her memory.

I don't mind telling you that I too get tears in my eyes sometimes.

As soon as the six jerrycans were full, my mother ordered the bellboy to take them all to the coach.

'Impossible,' the bellboy replied.

Nothing was impossible to my mother. And so, a moment later, the bellboy ferried the luggage over in the wheelchair belonging to the Indian man who'd helped them earlier that morning. It required seven trips. The coach was delayed by half an hour. The bellboy wouldn't hack it at Mumbai Central station either.

The driver was waiting in front of the coach with the passenger list. It was a different man this time. He put a squiggle after Ashirwad's name. My mother's name wasn't on the list.

'That's right,' my mother said, and urged Ashirwad to get on board ahead of her.

'So what about you?' the driver asked.

My mother looked over her shoulder one last time: at Lourdes, at the location of so many miracles — but not for her, not for her Ashirwad.

There was one consolation: the companion pass was still valid. With a smile on her face, my mother showed it to the driver.

THE SUPERINTENDENT

I was born at Western Railway's Jagjivan Ram Hospital in the city that was then called Bombay. At two minutes to three on the first morning of 1981, the obstetrician slipped his hands around me, catching me as I fell from fabulous forests of butterflies, and placed me in my mother's hands, in her arms. My eyes opened: small dark eyes with a blue sheen.

Here's what I've been told: I peed, I cried, and I tried to find the breast — in that order. Aunt Sharma and her daughter Neelam were present at my birth. Men weren't allowed in the delivery room. My father was 6,852 kilometres away, at the Van Ghent Barracks in Rotterdam. He was doing his national service, which he'd previously postponed, as first lieutenant with the military blood transfusion service. While I screamed open my lungs, my father worked on monoclonal antibodies against the house dust mite.

Aunt Sharma's husband phoned the barracks in Rotterdam. Uncle Sharma, that is. Somewhere halfway something went wrong: birds on the line — twittering sparrows. At one end, in the scorching heat of Bombay, Uncle Sharma announced the arrival of a son; in the harsh winter at the other end, I became a girl. My father was thrilled with the news. After two sons, he finally had a daughter. And her name would be Eva Maria van der Kwast. The name had been chosen months ago. Congratulations from the officers, from men in green, hugging and drinking sparkling wine they'd smuggled in. Birth announcement cards were ordered: handmade paper with an illustration of a stork carrying a pink-and-white check cloth.

Then came the second phone call: my mother from the hot city. There was screeching in the background — my screeching. Birds flew up from the line.

My father asked how things were going, how Eva Maria was doing.

'Who?' An arrow shot up the long line.

'Our Eva, our dear daughter. Oh, I can't tell you how pleased I am.'

'Ernest,' my mother said curtly. This name had also been picked long ago; this time my parents were well-prepared. *Ernest Roelof Arend van der Kwast*. A small being with wrinkles and creases, little hands and feet, and a willy. In a word: a boy.

'Oh,' came the response from the other end.

Perhaps it was the same surprise my father experienced at the birth of my eldest brother. He couldn't get his head around it yet.

'A son.' Another arrow. It hit the bull's eye this time, and a pink cloud burst.

I screamed in confirmation. Here I was, here was *Ernest*.

My father cleared his throat. He mentioned the birth announcement card that had been dispatched to the printer's. It said Eva Maria, in curly letters, and featured my data: 01-01-1981, 02:58, 3,254 grams.

It took a while for the scale of the disaster to sink in at the other end. Later, my mother would tell me that during this silence she considered her options, the potential ways of undoing the catastrophe. The birth announcement cards were being printed; she wouldn't be able to recoup the costs. Maybe they could swap *me* — for a girl. In that case, they could go ahead and use the cards.

'Everybody in India wants a son,' my mother said years later. 'We had three.'

We were arguing, as we did nearly every day. But this was something I hadn't heard before. I was lost for words.

'We could have easily swapped you for a girl. Plenty of choice.'

It sounded like a missed opportunity. My father would be better off as a rat in Delhi; I was convinced I would've been better off as a boy in Bombay.

'Are you still there?' my father asked from Rotterdam in 1981, in a barracks where men were fighting dust mites.

You bet my mother was still there. How could my father have been so stupid?! Since when was he entitled to do anything other than breathe? She began to shout and swear in Hindi. If there were any birds left on the line, they'd be dropping dead with fright now.

When the contractions started coming at ten-minute intervals, my mother drove to the Jagjivan Ram Hospital with her sister and her niece. Out in the street, firecrackers were exploding, and flowers of gold burst open against the dark sky. These fireworks had now burned up, but in a white house in a Bombay suburb, a blazing row continued for a long time.

I spent the first few weeks of my life in Uncle Sharma's house, amid limestone walls and delicate light, where the mornings began in the middle of the night.

There are stories — fragments of stories, really. I'm a restless baby and sleep little. I cry and shriek a lot. The family — Aunt Sharma's children, my brothers, and my mother — have nicknamed me *Tutto baby*.

That's all that's been passed down. Those days are shrouded in a milky haze for me. I try to see more, to use my imagination to turn the fragments into proper stories. But everything is so small: my own arms and legs, my hands and feet. There's nothing really, except movement and sound, hunger and thirst. Maybe that's the way it should be: the first few pages of life unwritten, blank as the oblivion of which we drink. Words are inappropriate — too big, and too heavy. Stones creating large circles in the water.

A month after my birth, the suitcases were packed again. Two taxis pulled up in front of the door: one for our luggage, one for us. During the last couple of days, my mother had been combing the shops in search of things that cost tenfold in the Netherlands: pans, scouring pads, tubes of toothpaste, toilet paper, and — of course — more suitcases to fit everything in.

Taxis were also cheaper than they were in the Netherlands, but they were against my mother's religion — a faith that always decreed the cheapest alternative, in this case the bus. 'Walking is even cheaper,' my mother once said. 'But that's just an illusion. Because if you walk, you need more food. And your shoes suffer more wear and tear, too.'

My uncle had booked the taxis. Uncle Sharma and my mother were poles apart. He spent his money on expensive clothes, ate out quite often, and *always* travelled by taxi. Four years later, during our first visit after my birth, I walked straight up to Uncle Sharma and rummaged around in his pockets, but I couldn't find the holes my mother had told me about.

It was a nine-hour flight, straight through the

dark, through the void. I drank from the breast and forgot everything that lay behind me. A story lost.

Upon arrival in the Netherlands, we were met by a white man in a green uniform: my father. I was asleep when I was thrust into his arms. But not for long, if my mother is to be believed. As soon as I smelled the stench of corpses, I started crying.

'They're dust mites,' my father said.

To which my mother replied: 'Why don't you carry the suitcases.'

Over Easter, the whole family spent a night at the Van Ghent Barracks. The barracks were deserted; my father was the duty officer. By now the house mite had bitten the dust, and the battle was on with a Chinese variant of the IgE molecule. The Cold War had the world in its grip.

Family members weren't allowed to stay over at the barracks, but my mother insisted that my father had a sleepless night at Easter. I wasn't one of those babies who sleep through the night after only three months. I was one of those babies who drive their parents to distraction. Perhaps I was a bomb even then; a bomb that would one day blow apart our family. As the Polish poet Czesław Miłosz puts it: 'When a writer is born into a family, the family is finished.'

That night, from Easter Sunday into Monday, my parents decided not to expand their brood. The total would remain at three — three sons — even though three is an unlucky number in India. Three is a harbinger of doom, of ruin. When we were children, our school lunchboxes would always contain either two or four sandwiches, and we were never allowed to play noughts and crosses. But at the Van Ghent Barracks, in the dead of night, my mother announced resolutely: 'Three's enough! Three's fine!'

Perhaps this exclamation, these words, ought to preface the written pages of my life. From now on, it can rain stones, since the wind has already disturbed the water surface. With the world on high alert, the imagination conjures up disaster scenarios.

My fantasy adds the innocent explosions of a sneezing fit. The entire barracks may have been free of house dust mites, but that didn't stop Ashirwad from sneezing through the night. Only Johan slept the sleep of the innocent, humming softly, far away in the land of dreams. I probably owed my life to him. He was the kind of baby, the kind of child, of which you wouldn't mind another ten. But then I came along: not the gift from God, but the number three, spelling doom, ruin.

For sixteen months, I sucked the breast that soothed and nourished me. Then my mother called it a day. She tried to keep me away from her breast by daubing sambal chilli paste on her nipples, but as a half-Indian I liked it *with* sambal, too. She finally weaned me off with toothpaste, squeezed from a tube purchased in Bombay. The thick, white paste was something we had plenty of. It was as bitter as rhubarb.

I greeted solid food with my mouth shut, lips pressed tightly together. Carrots, fennel, beetroot — I wouldn't have any of it. Ashirwad ate everything I didn't touch, the way he'd do later on as well, when I reached the terrible twos and threes and the horrible fours. Maybe that's why he's the tallest of us all.

The only food I ate willingly as a child was mango. There are images of this — the first distinct images. Memories.

The same limestone walls, the same delicate light. But this time the haze isn't made of milk, but of smoke: a whirling ribbon, traced in the air by an invisible hand; mysterious, floating lines.

Uncle Sharma was the only man we knew, far and wide, who smoked Benson & Hedges cigarettes. He bought them off a stranded British officer, who had them shipped over especially from the United Kingdom each month. Rumour had it that the officer lived off the proceeds of the cigarettes my uncle bought. He chain-smoked them. In fact, sometimes Uncle Sharma smoked two cigarettes at once. Absent-mindedness or wistfulness — it must have been one or the other. It happened when his eyes alighted on something in the distance and furrows appeared in his forehead. With his cigarette smouldering in the ashtray, his right hand would slip down to his trouser pocket, pull out the white packet of Benson & Hedges, tap out another cigarette, and light it. Uncle Sharma would inhale deeply and exhale the smoke through his O-shaped mouth. When his gaze unlocked from the distance and the lines in his forehead relaxed, his free hand would take the cigarette from the ashtray again and bring it to his mouth, and so, smiling, he'd take a drag from one cigarette, and a drag from the other.

My mother hated my uncle's habit. We weren't allowed anywhere near him. 'Smoking is dangerous,' she told us. 'It can kill you.' But all that's prohibited, all that's not allowed, is beguiling. And so I'd stand beside the chair in which Uncle Sharma sat, in which he stared into the distance and smoked one cigarette after another. My two brothers stood next to me. Together, we tried to read the white, whirling lines in the air, the surtitles of his thoughts.

On one occasion, I managed to snatch a cigarette from the ashtray. We ran away as fast as we could, like cowboys who've captured a treasure from the Red Indians. Uncle Sharma seemed oblivious, and simply pulled the packet of Benson & Hedges out of his pocket and lit a new cigarette.

I handed the cigarette to Ashirwad. It might be less of a shock if he were killed. He stuck it in his mouth, but no smoke emerged.

'You need to make an O with your lips,' I said.

Ashirwad opened his mouth wide, and the cigarette fell to the floor.

Johan picked it up again. 'It's gone out,' he said.

Then, out of the blue, we heard my mother's footsteps. I ran off at once. Ashirwad followed. Johan stayed put, the cigarette in his hand. While hiding in the garden, I heard my mother yelling, and Johan bawling. He got *tikkie*. Johan is also taller than me; he was the one who always got my thrashings.

When I returned to Uncle Sharma's chair, he wiggled his index finger at me. 'Tutto baby,' he said. 'Very naughty.' Then he cut me a slice of mango. Although it was too big, I stuck it all into my mouth at once. With the juice running down my face, I watched the ribbons in the air grow thinner and wispier until they dissolved completely. What words, what lines were hidden in that transparent script? What hand was writing them?

Even now, I experience the same enchantment, making me want to peek behind the curtain of smoke. By now, thousands of lines have been written — sentences that form a story, a life in the air. This is what I see, what I read, what I inhale:

Abhimanyu Sharma was born on 5 September 1928 in Bijnor, a small town in the state of Uttar Pradesh, a long way from Bombay. His father was a cobbler, his mother looked after the children. Abhimanyu was also a third son, but he was followed by four more daughters. His childhood was made of sun, dust, and rice. That's all there was — poverty with no prospect of escape, unless you had dreams.

Once a month, a man with a film projector travelled to Bijnor from the big city. The man wore white trousers and white shirts, and he had flashy rings on each of his fingers. He cut a flamboyant figure in this barren landscape. Chairs were set up in front of the wall of the police station in large, semi-circular rows. The projector was hoisted onto the roof of the house opposite — an event that attracted more spectators than a wedding between a doctor's son and a judge's daughter. All the children in the neighbourhood looked on with bated breath as the contraption was winched up with a rope, and when the first images, blurry and faded by the sun, appeared on the wall, they knew: there was life outside Bijnor. There was a way out.

The waiting commenced: for the sun to go down; for the sky to go red and then purple; for the dark-blue hour when all colour slowly drains from things. And then it was dark. Every month, it took an eternity. Yet the waiting brought joy to the village. Those who wait know why they're alive.

At the age of four, Abhimanyu saw his first film: *Cinema Girl*. He was sitting on a hill, 100 metres from the wall. He didn't see much — perhaps only the magic of cinema: moving images and beautiful people. He'd never forget the face of Prithviraj

Kapoor — the actor my mother was to look after on his deathbed, but who was then projected onto the wall of Bijnor police station, incredibly handsome and forever young.

When Abhimanyu came home late that night, he was met by his mother. She smacked him until her hands hurt. Later, lying on the floor between two sisters, Abhimanyu couldn't sleep. But not because of his burning skin. He kept seeing Prithviraj Kapoor's face: a smile of pearly white teeth, jet-black hair with a perfectly straight parting. Abhimanyu wiped the tears from his face and combed his wet fingers through his hair, from left to right. A smile stole over his face. Abhimanyu Sharma had a dream.

The following morning, he was the first to wake. Sitting up with a jolt, he exclaimed: 'I'm going to be an actor!'

His little sisters rubbed their eyes and called him crazy.

The father woke up and asked irritably: 'What's going on?'

'Abhimanyu wants to be an actor,' one of the sisters said with a giggle.

'*Chup ho djao,*' their mother shouted.

Abhimanyu remembered her hard hands and decided to keep quiet. He ate his rice and went out into the street. At the water pump, he stuck his head under the tap and combed his hair into a parting. Then he ran over to the man with the mirror. It cost one rupee to look at yourself.

'I'm going to be an actor,' Abhimanyu said. 'I'll pay you a hundred rupees later.'

The man shook his head.

'A thousand rupees.'

For an instant, the mirror was brought out and reflected Abhimanyu's face: his wet, black hair, his smile with the three missing teeth.

For the rest of the day — and indeed, throughout the days of dust and sunshine — he walked back and forth to the water pump with this smile on his face.

When, a month later, the man with the film projector came to wake the village again, Abhimanyu was the first to put down a chair on the square in front of the police station wall. Older boys kept chasing him away, but he kept coming back.

'I'm going to be an actor!' Abhimanyu exclaimed. 'I'm going to be just as famous as Prithviraj Kapoor.'

People laughed; people always laughed.

That evening, he saw the film from the roof of a house where he'd managed to secure a spot among the older boys. That night, he was given another spanking. Abhimanyu cried and begged for mercy, but his mother's hands were merciless. Maybe he pictured her hands, later, all those years later, when his eyes alighted on something in the distance.

And then there was sound. It came from large black boxes brought along by the man with the film projector. During the day, Abhimanyu had helped to put down chairs and had gazed in astonishment at the boxes that were lifted from large wooden crates. He wanted to lift one too, but felt a hand on his shoulder — a hand with a golden ring on each finger.

'Later,' the film-projector man said. 'When you're all grown up.'

It was the first time he spoke to the boy. Abhimanyu combed his fingers through his hair, from left to right, and flashed a smile that could lose its final milk tooth any moment now.

The man smiled, too, and pulled a photo from his breast pocket. It had a wavy border.

'Prithviraj Kapoor!' Abhimanyu exclaimed. Only afterwards did he notice that there was a black scribble on it: the actor's autograph. He almost cried with happiness.

As soon as the stars appeared in the sky, the film came on: *Alam Ara* (The Light of the World). It was the first Indian film with sound: talking, singing, and dancing. When it was shown in Bombay, the police had to step in to calm the audience. Likewise, in Bijnor people didn't know what hit them. Spectators looked around in surprise; some got up and went in search of the sound, while others burst into a thunderous applause. The odd person stuck his fingers in his ears. Abhimanyu loved the songs and stared open-mouthed at the dancing actors. Unable to stop himself, he began to move, too. He lifted his feet and shook his hips. He was dancing on the roof.

The following day, the cheerful melodies from *Alam Ara* were everywhere. It was as if Bijnor had become an altogether different place, set in a different world. On every street corner, in every shop, in every house, the film's opening song, 'De De Khuda Ke Naam Pe Pyaare', could be heard. Abhimanyu sang it at home, too. It was sung all over India.

One by one, the family's daughters left home. They got married, had children, and gave them names they'd be yelling day and night in rooms and kitchens, at markets and squares, trying to make themselves heard over the street noise. But one day, those yells would no longer get through to the children, and these daughters would be all alone in the world.

Abhimanyu was seventeen when he left Bijnor with no more than a comb in his back pocket. He'd grown into a strapping lad. His brothers worked the land, walking twelve kilometres to the plot every morning before sunrise. They arrived back home in the evening, worn out and black with soil.

'Bombay,' the man with the film projector had said. 'That's where it's all happening; that's where you need to be going.' Abhimanyu wasn't the only Indian boy with dreams of the silver screen: millions had the same dream and were pursuing it. 'Go,' the man had told him. 'But if you do, go for it unreservedly. Even if it means you won't have anything to eat, no place to sleep, and nothing to fall back on as you sink deeper and deeper into despair. Either you really go for it, or you stay here and stop dreaming.'

His mother yelled his name on the platform — the last time he'd ever hear her voice. Abhimanyu Sharma was going, and he was really going for it.

Although he'd never lay eyes on his mother again, it was not so the other way around. Six years after his departure, one starry night in March, a wave of joy swept through Bijnor, from the front to the second, third, fourth row, all the way to the final row, and from there up to the roofs and hills before finally reaching the Sharma family home.

The film was stopped. And rewound. And then stopped again. His face was as big as the wall of the police station. 'Abhimanyu!' the people shouted with one voice. 'Abhimanyu!'

His mother was given a seat in the front row, from where she saw her son singing and dancing. Waterfalls of sound accompanied him, as did beautiful, bare-bellied women, princesses in glittering gold. 'Abhimanyu,' she muttered, and then the tears came because her voice would never reach him again.

But before he was to go through life talking, singing, and dancing, Abhimanyu went hungry and slept with countless others on the beaches of Dadar and Versova. Here, in these Bombay suburbs, they dreamed the same dream, the young men from all over India, the men who had all but drowned already.

In Bombay, Abhimanyu went to every casting and audition and tried to speak to every known director and important producer: Ardeshir Irani, V. Shantaram, Sohrab Modi — big names at Bollywood's final resting place.

Again, there are stories. This time, they're not just fragments, but an epic narrative. My uncle, the man who announced my arrival against the backdrop of bird song, is thought to have been discovered by Gum Dutt, the actor, director, and producer, living legend, and bulk consumer of women and alcohol. The young Abhimanyu is rumoured to have made an 'indelible impression' in the studios of the Prabhat Film Company, where Gum Dutt worked as an assistant director at the time. The epic, sung by nephews and nieces and a large chorus of aunts and neighbouring women, also praises his smile 'without a single tooth missing' and 'the gleaming black hair with a parting as straight as the fold in *The Times of India*'. But IMDb, the internet movie database, doesn't list Abhimanyu Sharma as one of the cast of *Pyaasa* or *Kaagaz Ke Phool*, both Gum Dutt classics. As I watch these films, I try to identify my uncle among the sea of actors in mass scene after mass scene. But they all look alike: identical smiles, identical partings.

The last time I saw Uncle Sharma was in Rotterdam, on Tiberiaslaan, during the summer of 1990. Our family had borrowed a stack of videotapes from the neighbours across the street to get us through the long evenings. One of the tapes was *Indiana Jones and the Temple of Doom*. We watched the film out on the patio, with the extension cord snaking across the flagstones, and the sounds from the adjacent tennis courts — balls being thwacked back and forth — in the background. And over and above that, the snoring of my mother and her sister, Aunt Sharma. The affliction appears to run in the family, although my mother's sister also rabidly denies that she snores.

Uncle Sharma was sitting next to me on the couch. His hair was thinner now, and slicked back. Yet his clothes were as white as ever, and he still smoked the same Benson & Hedges cigarettes. A veil of smoke enveloped him wherever he went. He'd given me a signed photograph and told me it was worth a lot of money — not in Dutch guilders, but in Indian rupees. The currency wasn't on the exchange rate board at the local bank.

Indiana Jones and the Temple of Doom is set in India, or rather, against a backdrop that's meant to depict India. It was actually filmed in Sri Lanka, because the filmmakers had been denied permission from the Indian government to shoot in North India. The authorities considered the script 'racist' and demanded all manner of revisions and the right to veto the final edit. But we didn't know that when we slid the videotape into the VCR.

It went wrong the moment the film started, when Indiana crashes in the Himalayas and the inhabitants of a remote village believe he's been sent by the Hindu god Shiva. Uncle Sharma shook his head. 'Indiana Jones sent by Shiva?' I heard him growl. 'Out of the question.' A little later, he jumped to his feet when the film showed people being offered to the goddess Kali. 'Out of the question,' he repeated. '*Completely* out of the question.' And he wagged his finger at the television screen when Indiana Jones grinned at the imminent danger. Then he sat down again and lit a cigarette.

Ashirwad woke my mother and her sister to say that he couldn't hear the film. Both denied they'd been asleep. 'I'm watching the film, too,' my mother said.

'You're snoring,' Ashirwad said. 'And so are you.' He pointed to Aunt Sharma.

'What's he saying?' she asked her sister in Hindi. My mother interpreted for her.

Aunt Sharma shook her head furiously and spat out a curse in Hindi, sounding like an old car that was having trouble starting.

Uncle Sharma weighed in: 'Ashirwad is right.'

'No, he's not,' shouted my mother. 'We don't snore.'

An object came flying over my head. For a moment I thought it was a tennis ball, but no, it was a slipper.

My father pressed the pause button on the remote. It had become impossible to watch the film. We had things to discuss first.

Aunt Sharma rattled off words to her husband that I was familiar with; the only Indian words I was familiar with. The vintage car had been started.

'You *are* snoring!' Ashirwad shouted. 'You *are* snoring!'

And who knows, perhaps the discussion would have gone on until well past midnight, had the VCR not spontaneously switched to 'play' again and the screen showed a severed monkey's head with an Indian man eating the brains.

Uncle Sharma jumped up from the couch again, and this time he went and stood in front of the television. He looked at us, stern like a teacher, and said: 'Out of the question.'

I don't remember the exact words of the monologue that followed, only the gist of it: India had a population of one billion, but of all those inhabitants, not a single one ate monkey brains. Ashirwad was the only one to react: 'My favourite food is snakies.'

Uncle Sharma refused to let it distract him. He stood in front of the television for at least another minute, rigid as a statue. Even the cigarette in his right hand seemed frozen in time; no ribbons of smoke came trailing out, as I remember it. Then he calmly walked inside and we watched the rest of the film without him.

The curtain, the veil of smoke, had opened. But perhaps the metaphor is wearing thin. The way Uncle Sharma had stood in front of the television is how I would first see him on celluloid during a Hindu festival. I recognised him instantly: the large physique, the smooth forehead, the slicked-back hair. He was playing 'Superintendent of Police' in *Janam Janam*, a drama that utilises the device of the flashback to dizzying effect, and in which Uncle Sharma makes a sudden appearance. He enters the film with measured, calm steps, looking authoritative and dignified. The scenes starring my uncle can be counted on the fingers of one hand, and they don't feature much dialogue. The Superintendent is economical with words. His presence is supposed to do the job; it's the presence of someone who can't be ignored. Halfway through the final scene, he folds his arms. Job done.

According to various family sources, Abhimanyu Sharma featured in more than 200 Bollywood films. But IMDb lists only 25, all post-1960. The time between 1945 and 1960 is eternal smoke. But those with enough imagination can also see him in films by Ardeshir Irani, V. Shantaram, and Sohrab Modi, dancing among a sea of actors, lost in the credits. My hand likes to add him.

(Sometimes I can picture myself in a film, one more recent, more modern, and even sweeter. In my arms, a slender, gorgeous woman with glittering jewellery around her ankles, arms, and neck. We twist and turn through streets and palaces. It's the life I missed out on, the actor I could have been had I been swapped for a girl: Eva Maria. This, too, is a story I'd like to write. It takes no effort on my part, as if the enchanting blue still covers my eyes and I always see more than meets the eye, and remember more than actually happened.)

Uncle Sharma would never become as famous as Prithviraj Kapoor, but he did play with all the great actors of his day. He was recognised in the street, and people often asked for his autograph — they even had him sign 100-rupee notes. In thousands of cities, the little boy from Bijnor appeared like a giant on the silver screen: sometimes in a police uniform, sometimes in a pristine white doctor's coat.

Indian cinema has a limited number of roles: the hero, the bad guy, the beauty, and the in-laws. These all come with an entourage, consisting largely of neurotic characters that talk nineteen to the dozen. What they say doesn't really matter. Then there are the countless dancers who lip-sync as if their lives depend on it. But each film also has an actor playing a big shot, an influential person, a bigwig: Uncle Sharma.

In the films I order online, and that sometimes take up to seven months to arrive, I see him as 'Superintendent of Police' on three occasions, as well as in the role of 'Prosecuting lawyer', 'Doctor Sharma',

'Inspector Sharma', and 'Diwan's guest'. In other films, which I get hold of through relatives, he plays roles such as 'Hotel manager', 'Construction superintendent', 'Judge Sharma', and 'Restaurant owner'.

There's always a problem between the lead characters, which prompts my uncle to walk on out of nowhere — always with the same steady gait, the same solemn gaze. He listens to the other characters, nods quietly, and then adjudicates, arranges a separate table, or prescribes medication. That done, he folds his arms. The *deus ex machina* of Indian film has accomplished his task.

After *Indiana Jones and the Temple of Doom*, we never met again, although we came very close in 2001. Uncle Sharma owned a flat in London and had invited us to stay with him and his wife for a week. A free holiday certainly appealed to my mother.

Uncle Sharma's daughter Neelam came to pick us up at the station. My entire immediate family had come along, so we set a new luggage record. Neelam insisted on taking a cab, but my mother thought it was too expensive. First she got into an argument with the cab driver, who refused to lower his price, then with Neelam, who shouted that we weren't in India.

Perhaps Uncle Sharma could have intervened as the big shot who suddenly appears on screen. But he'd stopped acting by then. Seven hours later, we were back home. My father collapsed on the doorstep, a holdall around his neck.

The final act: 27 April 2003, Leicester Square Theatre, London. Actors from Mumbai are performing a lavish show, talking, singing, and dancing in colourful outfits, on a magnificent stage. Uncle Sharma and his daughter are in the front row — by special invitation from the actors. There's a 300-strong audience in the theatre, virtually all Indians. They're singing, clapping, and emoting along.

At the end of the show, Neelam feels her father's head on her shoulder. Uncle Sharma has fallen asleep. It's not uncommon for him these days to fall asleep during films and plays. It all becomes too much for him. But when the audience rises for a standing ovation, he doesn't wake up. Uncle Sharma remains seated, his face immobile, his arms folded.

'Jeena yahan marna yahan,' Indians say. 'You live here, you die here.' Uncle Sharma lived and died on stage.

Then the curtain falls.

THE INDIAN DREAM

There were seven trophies on my mother's bedside table: old iron cups, which time had robbed of their sheen and covered in dark rust as well as a thick layer of dust. The biggest cup took pride of place in the middle; it had long, slender handles, while the concavity itself was as deep and wide as a helmet. The other trophies sat in its shadow, in descending order of size. The smallest ones had lids, which, if you lifted them up, released the smell of soil, of summery soil.

There were no engraved metal plaques on the trophies' wooden bases. All information about provenance — date, location, discipline — was missing. For all I knew, they could be antique drinking goblets, once touched by my ancestors' lips. In fact, as children, we tried to drink from the empty cups and ended up sipping dust. We cried.

My mother polished the trophies with a cloth, but the rust refused to budge and the dust returned

— the way dust returns, always and everywhere. The only place it didn't get was underneath the trophies, beneath their wooden bases. These small squares were so clean they seemed to sparkle. Now and again, I'd lift all the trophies from the bedside table and gaze at the emergent black lacquer — a series of miniature lakes — in the hope of ascertaining the trophies' origins. Sometimes I'd see an ancient woman in those depths, drinking with trembling hands: my mother's mother's mother.

Not much later, the world changed forever, and everything that once appeared to have depth became hard and flat. It was like a slap in the face: wake up!

The trophies came from India, where, as a girl, my mother had run across the playing fields of Queen Victoria Girls Inter College in Agra. This is where her bare feet had dashed across the warm soil, the loose sand. This was the smell under the lids. She was known for getting off to a flying start. Nobody could hit the ground running like my mother.

'I had the best ears,' my mother told us. 'And the fastest legs.'

My father claimed she was often on her way before the starting signal had even sounded. 'The difference between a flying start and a false start is open to discussion in India,' he whispered in my ear.

My mother still had good ears. She took off a slipper

and used it to hit my father on the head. Then she said: 'There was no such thing as a starting signal in those days.' This prompted her to tell us about the man at the starting line, an official in a white sleeveless jumper who enunciated his words very carefully. Six words: 'On your marks, get set, go!'

My mother sprinted off wearing only a single slipper, right through the living room and dining room. It's a good thing the sliding doors were open. When she got to the end of the dining room, she threw her arms up in the air. Then she walked back with a smile on her face.

'Let's do it together now,' she said. 'A competition.'

She put her other slipper back on and took up the starting position. I followed her example.

My father was expected to officiate, speaking the six words the way the official in India had done, but wearing a tatty sweater, because my father didn't own a white sleeveless jumper. New clothes were wasted on him, according to my mother. On Saturdays, there was underwear on the washing line with holes big enough for birds to fly through. One day it would probably be mended by an Indian tailor.

'Theo,' my mother said.

Surmising that he might end up doing something wrong, my father didn't want to be an official. But whenever my mother uttered his first name, he knew he had no choice. His name was synonymous with a death threat.

'On your marks …' my father said, somewhat reluctantly. 'Get set.' And then: 'Go!'

And off I went, but my mother was already at the sliding doors. She won the sprint by a considerable margin — the length of the dining room.

My father shook his head, but was afraid to protest.

I was six when my parents first took me to PAC, an athletics club in Rotterdam. It was a Saturday morning in the 1980s. The trainer went by the unusual name of Freek Ruigrok and he wore a purple-and-yellow tracksuit. My mother had given me shorts to wear. I was the only boy in my age group with black socks.

We ran a lap around the dark-red cinder track, Freek Ruigrok in front, the little ones following behind in an ever-lengthening trail. Some children had been sent because their parents thought they might benefit from exercise — boys with fat calves and chubby faces, their shoes dragging across the coarse cinders. And then there were the children who'd been registered for athletics because it was good for the parents — boys who couldn't or wouldn't sit still, who had to run, jump, and bounce around. I belonged to the latter group. My body fizzed with energy; food colourings had a disastrous effect.

'Why don't you get him to run ten laps,' my father had said to the trainer. 'That way he'll be a bit calmer at home.' Now he and my mother were sitting on the grass beside the track. It looked like a peaceful scene — from a distance, anyway. My young parents enjoying the peace and quiet.

My father was trying to read an article, probably one about prostates. He'd recently become a prostate cancer specialist. He tried to read an article on the topic every weekend, but my mother wouldn't let him work at home. And so he usually read the articles on the sly, on the toilet. Whenever he spent too long on the toilet, my mother would press her ear to the door. 'I hear papers,' she'd say. 'I hear rustling!'

'I have rights, too,' came the reply from the other side. 'I'm allowed to do a number two.'

My mother would sit down on the floor, pointing her nose to the narrow opening between the threshold and the bottom of the door. 'I can't smell a thing!'

'I'm constipated,' my father replied. 'Leave me alone.'

'You're working,' my mother yelled. 'You're reading an article.'

'No, I'm not!'

My mother banged her fists on the door. 'Get out!'

'When I'm done, when I've taken a shit.'

Sometimes it took up to half an hour before the toilet was flushed and the door was carefully opened. My mother had been waiting all that time, growing more impatient and more irate by the minute. She blocked my father's path and ordered him to spread his arms and legs so she could search him.

'I took a shit,' my father shouted. 'I'm not a criminal.'

My mother frisked my father's body — up and down, front and back. She would have made a good border-control officer in the Eastern bloc. There were two scenarios: either she'd feel the papers beneath his clothes, or she'd find them behind the toilet bowl, hidden under the waste pipe. The conclusion was always the same. My mother would tear up the article over the toilet. My father, on his knees, would fish the snippets out of the bowl.

Such scenes make an indelible impression on a child.

Likewise, whenever my mother was in the kitchen, or making beds, or even just looking the other way, my father tried to read and annotate articles about prostate cancer. He rarely succeeded. There were times my mother was so enraged she tried to eat an article.

I waved at my parents from the other side of the athletics track. I was running right behind Freek Ruigrok, almost at the front. My mother waved back. She'd got up and was urging me to go faster.

'*Jaldi*! *Jaldi*!' rang out across the central grass area. Faster! Faster!

But the instant she noticed my father reading an article, she lunged at his papers, like a bird of prey swooping down on its victim.

This time, it was my father's voice that rang out across the grass: 'Help! Help!'

It was futile, since my mother had already run off with the article. She bolted across the grass and ripped it up over the nearest bin.

(Now, more than 20 years later, my father is still doing research into prostate cancer, at Toronto's University Health Network. He's a leading researcher and publishes regularly in major medical journals. There's no breakthrough yet; the cure for prostate cancer is slow to materialise. Sometimes I think a remedy could've been found a long time ago, had it not been for my mother ripping up, flushing, or devouring all of those articles. I shudder to think of all those men who died prematurely or who became impotent. Maybe my mother doesn't mind, cruel hangman that she is.)

After that first training session, my father didn't come along again. But my mother never missed one during my first year. She was more fanatic than any football dad. Every Saturday morning and every Wednesday afternoon, she'd take me to the athletics track and encourage me vociferously from the sidelines. After that first training session, Freek Ruigrok had taken to calling me Jaldi, a name that the other kids would soon adopt and that would stick until the age of 21.

My first competition was PAC's club championship. The programme for the boys aged six to seven consisted of four elements: the 40-metre sprint; a children's version of shotput, with a foam ball; long jump; and the 600 metres. I was a little nervous, but it was nothing compared to my mother's agitation. She was full of questions, and her hands were shaking something terrible, so much so that she couldn't pin the race number on the back of my orange club shirt. I felt a pin prick in my back and was about to get angry when I saw the tears in her eyes.

'Mama,' is what I would say now. 'Calm down — there's no need to cry. I know you're proud and that you won't be later on, but that you love me because I'm your child. Dry your tears, mother, and give me a hug. We'll hold each other across time.'

In the end, Jurjen Coenen's mother helped us with the race number. Jurjen also lived on Jericholaan, but he was a year older than me. He was competing in the next category up, and by the close of day he'd have set a new club record on the 1,000 metres. Later, when we were both competing in the Juniors, he was to be my rival. Or rather: my mother's rival.

First on the programme for the youngest athletes was the 40-metre sprint. The distance felt interminable at the time, but now, with the benefit of hindsight, it's just a quick dash, a scratch on one's memory, practically invisible.

My mother escorted me to the starting line. For the umpteenth time, she asked me if I knew which series and which track I was in. I nodded: third series, track four. Then she pulled up my t-shirt and stuffed it back into my shorts. Had it not been for her trembling hands, she'd have retied my laces, too.

It was touching, my mother's fretting. But embarrassing, too. While the boys in the second series were getting ready, my mother asked me: 'Did you have a wee?'

I had a sneaking suspicion I'd done something wrong, so I quickly shook my head.

'Ernest,' she said, in the same menacing tone she'd say my father's name.

The toilets over in the canteen were too far away; I'd miss my series if I went.

'You can't win on a full bladder,' my mother said, and pointed to a tree beside the track.

I tried to make my way there as inconspicuously as possible, but was spotted by two other children in my age group. So before you could count to three, everybody on and around the track knew I was pissing behind a tree. There was laughter — the kind of laughter that cuts through a child's soul.

'Take no notice,' my mother said, and adjusted my t-shirt again. Taking no notice, especially not of other people, was my mother's guiding principle in life, a maxim she herself lived by.

Then the starting signal rang out, and off we went. '*Jaldi!*' my mother screamed. '*Jaldi! Jaldi!*' She egged me on with the fervour of an entire Indian family: father, mother, two sons, numerous daughters.

I may not have got off to a flying start, but I was still the first to cross the chalk finishing line. With my chest out, as Freek Ruigrok had taught me. My mother was standing on the sidelines, ready to congratulate me — she'd sprinted 40 metres as well. But first we had to retrace our steps, backwards, so the members of the jury could see the numbers on our backs. This was the era of stopwatches, of beeps, of pencil, paper, and eraser.

'You see,' my mother said. 'Weeing helps.' She wrapped me in her warm, strong arms. Her eyes were filled with tears. 'Always listen to your mother,' she whispered. That was her advice to me. If I lived by that rule, everything would be all right.

I made two invalid attempts in the long jump. The third jump earned me a fourth place, but I slipped from first to second position in the intermediate rankings. My mother, meanwhile, had been banned from the track for harassing the officials. She took exception to my jumps being declared invalid.

'He's so young,' she said to the official sitting on the chair by the take-off board after my first jump. 'And he's trying so hard.'

After my second jump, she pushed down the red flag and grabbed the white flag out of the official's hands and raised it up into the air. And when the other officials refused to measure the distance, my mother walked into the sandpit with measuring steps before solemnly declaring: 'Four metres, 70 centimetres' — a distance that would've been a club record, if not a new world record for the six to seven age category, if there was one.

Eventually my mother became an official herself, but not before first failing the diploma of the Royal Dutch Athletics Federation seven times. She was determined to become an official not for altruistic reasons, but because of the packed lunches. If you officiated at an athletics meet, you were given a packed lunch and a few tea or coffee vouchers — an arrangement that was just as attractive as a supermarket bargain.

As an official, my mother always tried to swap her drinks vouchers for packed lunches. Before the first part of the programme got underway, she'd speak to all the other officials and inform them of the exchange rate. Every now and then, she'd miss an invalid throw because she was engaged in a heated discussion with a colleague about the maximum number of vouchers she was prepared to swap for a packed lunch.

Where my mother goes, trade follows.

Every competition day, my brothers and my father were expected to come to the athletics track at noon, and we were each given a packed lunch. For this — for a transparent plastic bag with white rolls, each spread with a thick layer of margarine and filled with ham, cheese, and paté; for currant buns and apples — my mother pressed stopwatches, measured distances, and placed bars at the correct height. We scoffed it all greedily enough, though — we knew we wouldn't be getting anything else at home later.

❈

I became club champion in my age category, having won both the ball throw and the 600 metres. During the latter event, my mother ran nearly the entire distance on the grass beside the track. Some mothers stared, unable to believe their eyes; others just shook their heads in pity. But my mother took no notice. On the final stretch, she kept chanting: *'Jaldi! Jaldi!'*

The podium was made of three orange oil drums of different heights. The announcement of my name was followed by applause that continued until my mother finally stopped. I climbed the tallest oil drum and waited for the chairman to come forward. He began by handing out the prizes to the boys standing next to me on the podium. Their names are buried under thousands of other names in my memory; they're impossible to retrieve from oblivion. Then the chairman stepped sideways and stood right in front of me.

My first prize, my first trophy: club champion, boys aged six to seven, 1987. I searched for my mother in the crowd and found her laughing and beaming. It was the first occasion I saw her happy, like other mothers. It was as if time jumped forward a little, stirred by a sudden summery gust of wind.

When I stood by her side, she told everyone I'd inherited my talent from her and her sisters. 'We were all gifted athletes,' she told the chairman. 'We were always winning trophies and medals. Barefoot.' At that she showed the calloused skin on her feet, unsolicited

— something other mothers would never do, however exuberant they might be.

Back on Jericholaan, I was told to show my prize to the neighbours, even those across the street. Everybody had to know that I'd become club champion. The next day, my mother came with me to school and insisted that I show off my trophy in every single classroom. Miss Bierenbroodspot, who was usually incredibly strict, was afraid to say no. It must have been something in my mother's eyes — bloodthirstiness, probably.

In the years that followed, I won countless prizes, and they always had to be shown to as many people as possible. Showing off is quintessentially Indian. I remember the many long car journeys home after competitions in various parts of the Netherlands. Back in Rotterdam, my mother would wake everybody up so we could get ready to assume our positions. As soon as our house came in sight, she'd yell: 'Now!' My father would have to slam on the horn and drive up and down Jericholaan, and later Tiberiaslaan, several times, until all the neighbours had seen us: my father squeezing the steering wheel, my brothers laughing, my mother waving as though she were the Queen, and me, forced to hold my medal or trophy out of the window.

And then one day an old man in a red suit turned up on our doorstep. He had a carefully tended moustache and introduced himself as Mr Kumar. Thinking he was a door-to-door salesman, someone with Miracle Wipes in his suitcase, I tried to close the door. But then Mr Kumar pointed to the gold-emblazoned emblem near his chest: *Athletics Federation of India*.

A little later, Mr Kumar was sitting at the table in our living room. He held his tea cup in both hands and took a sip every now and then. As a rule, nobody was let into our home. Schoolfriends, acquaintances, my father's colleagues: they all had to wait outside. My mother was ashamed of the mess. Her compulsive hoarding had reached new heights after she'd acquired a load of surplus extractor hoods. We needed a psychologist more than a Miracle Wipe. Mr Kumar either didn't notice the mess, or he thought it was perfectly normal to see a tower of VCRs in the living room. Perhaps his wife was impossible, too, and all Indian women were committed collectors.

My mother talked to Mr Kumar in Hindi, interspersed with the occasional English word: 'champion', 'javelin', 'free lunch'. I wanted to get up from the table, but my mother stopped me. Mr Kumar had come for me, she said.

'All the way from Bombay,' the representative of the Indian Athletics Federation added.

My birthplace. I smiled.

Mr Kumar also knew that I'd been born in Bombay; it was more or less the reason for his visit. But I wasn't to find out until later.

When the tea was finished, we headed upstairs.

First off, my mother showed Mr Kumar her own prizes, the seven iron trophies on her bedside cabinet.

'I remember,' Mr Kumar said, while lifting the biggest cup off the bedside cabinet. 'Lucknow, 1957.'

My mother nodded. For a split second I thought I saw tears, but it was a shimmer, a film over her eyes, as if she was looking through the dust, through the rust, and saw the shiny trophy she'd held aloft as a young girl.

'I was the fastest among thousands of girls,' my mother whispered.

'On your marks, get set, go!' Mr Kumar said, and winked.

I was expecting the story that went with the wink, but Mr Kumar put the cup back, in the exact same spot, on the dark, dust-free square — a seal on the past.

Then we made our way to my room. My desk was a mess; it was full of open textbooks and exercise books, apple cores, and chocolate wrappers. I was in my penultimate year of secondary school, and in two weeks' time I was sitting my first mock exams. I had another 500 lines of ancient Greek to read (*Histories* by Herodotus). It was an undertaking I wished I could run away from, to the athletics track, but my mother kept a close eye on me. In fact, she never lost sight of me.

Mr Kumar made a beeline for my trophy cabinet. My father had knocked together a special structure with a glass door, so my medals, trophies, and cups wouldn't get covered in dust. Every weekend, I opened the door and put in a new prize. My collection had almost outgrown the cabinet.

'May I?' Mr Kumar asked.

I nodded.

He opened the glass door and picked up a heavy medal. It was the first prize of a multi-event in Gorinchem. I'd begun to specialise in the throwing events: shotput, javelin, and discus. I excelled at the latter. The distance I'd thrown in Gorinchem had earned me a track record and a high position in the rankings for that year, 1998. The Dutch championships were taking place in Amsterdam in July. It was a lot more appealing to me than my Greek exam.

Mr Kumar picked up a trophy and held it close to his face. The reflective cup distorted his features into a caricature with enormous eyebrows. He tried to read the inscription on the metal plate on the base. He produced some guttural sounds, followed by: 'Most interesting.' The trophy was replaced. Mr Kumar had to stand on tiptoe to see the top shelf — the shelf with the largest trophies.

'Very nice,' he said. 'Very, *very* nice.' He made it sound as if he was interested in purchasing the prizes.

I told him the story behind every cup: the date, the location, the discipline. Mr Kumar nodded continuously, and muttered a few lines in Hindi each time. The only word I understood was 'Bombay'. Mr Kumar was really pleased with my place of birth.

Then he said: 'I want to make you a very special offer.' His dark eyebrows appeared to momentarily detach from his face, to hover in the air.

Every country has its black page in history, a trauma it simply can't come to terms with. India's greatest collective trauma may well be athletics. The most recent Olympic accolade dates back to 1900, when Norman Pritchard won silver medals in the 200-metre sprint and the 200-metre hurdles. But Pritchard was Anglo-Indian. Exclude him, and the overall count is extremely sparse. In a word, it's nil.

India isn't exactly a high-flyer in other Olympic disciplines, either. The only sport in which the country does well is field hockey. The national team has won a total of eleven medals, including eight golds. The first individual gold wasn't achieved until 2008, in Beijing, by 25-year-old Abhinav Bindra, who won the '10-metre air rifle', and at a stroke became India's most eligible bachelor — according to his mother, that is.

Abhinav Bindra's win brought the total Olympic medal haul to eighteen, thereby equalling Uzbekistan.

A population of 1.1 billion, yet so few medals — it's a deep-seated trauma, not to mention a great mystery. Some researchers have made the link between poverty and the lack of success. Sport is a luxury available to few Indians. But Uzbekistan is also poor, other researchers argue. According to them, the problem lies with the Indian physique, which is unsuited to sports such as judo, athletics, swimming, gymnastics, rowing, and wrestling. The Indian physique really only lends itself to leisurely sports such as cricket, which isn't an Olympic discipline unfortunately.

The research notwithstanding, the Indian nation remains hopeful. And the flame of that hope was kindled by a statement by the minister of sport following the debacle of the 1996 Olympic Games: a single bronze medal. He announced on national television: 'We have plenty of talent, but it really needs to be nurtured.' This kickstarted a veritable manhunt for talent, one that continues to this day. Not long ago, the Ministry of Sport launched a project in the province of Tamil Nadu to find swimmers and gymnasts among the fishermen and street performers there. Tightrope-walkers are plucked off the street in the hope of beating China on the beam at the next Olympics.

Perhaps Mr Kumar was one of the first envoys from the Ministry of Sport in search of talent — all the way in Rotterdam. Mr Kumar's plan involved me taking on Indian nationality, which was possible thanks to my mother and my birth in Bombay. In exchange, I'd be given accommodation in Secunderabad, near the Gymkhana Ground, India's athletics Valhalla. A top European coach would be flown in as well.

Mr Kumar looked at me expectantly. He'd spoken rapidly, the smell of gold in his nostrils. In his eyes,

I was already the first Indian to win a track-and-field medal at the Olympics. A visit to the embassy in The Hague was all it would take. Perhaps there was a passport waiting for me already.

I thought of my exams. Here was my chance of escape.

But my mother didn't like the sound of Mr Kumar's offer. She shook her head and then pointed resolutely to my desk, to the open textbooks and exercise books. I couldn't leave. I had to listen to my mother. I had to learn Greek lines by heart.

Mr Kumar raised his voice and made angry gestures. He wasn't ready to give up his dream, the Indian dream.

There was no reaction from my mother. That's to say, not right there and then, not without a rolling pin handy.

I sat down at my desk and put a page of the *Histories* in front of me: the conversation between Solon and Croesus as to who is the happiest of all men. The exam was inescapable.

My mother beckoned for Mr Kumar to come with her. They left my room and walked down the stairs — nimble footsteps followed by a heavy tread. The kitchen door was opened, and not much later I heard my mother scream like a madwoman. Croesus wasn't the happiest of all men, and nor was Mr Kumar.

When I heard a loud crash, I ran downstairs. I saw Mr Kumar lying flat on the carpet in the living room.

After fleeing the kitchen, he'd bumped into the tower of VCRs. The carpet was littered with pieces of black casing and other components. My mother was busy picking them up and putting them into a plastic carrier bag — a lifetime's worth of work for a repairman in India.

I helped Mr Kumar up and escorted him to the front door. I had to hold him tight; he was trembling all over. My mother went on collecting bits of VCR as though nothing had happened.

On the doorstep, Mr Kumar burst into an incoherent and emotional monologue, shouting things about Queen Victoria Girls Inter College and about the Ahluwalia family, about my mother's sisters. I'd inherited my talent from Aunt Jasleen; I mustn't waste it. I mustn't listen to my mother, the way Jasleen had listened to her mother. In the end, all Mr Kumar said was: 'Jasleen, Jasleen, Jasleen.' Like a record that was stuck.

He walked down the street with his tail between his legs.

Inside, the carpet had been cleared. In the corner of the living room, a number of VCRs had been stacked on top of one another. My mother was sitting on the sofa, staring into space. She was sobbing quietly. I stood behind her, not moving.

After a long time, my mother said: 'Aunt Jasleen is a renowned lung specialist.' Then she sent me up to my room, to my desk.

My feet shot up the stairs. At the top, I didn't go straight to my own room, but instead opened the door to my parents' bedroom. The top drawer of the bedside cabinet, below the trophies, held old photos — really old ones, from before I was born.

There was one photo of the entire Ahluwalia family, which had survived, which hadn't been lost to history, buried under earth and rubble, scraps and shards. My mother had showed me that photo once. 'This is my family,' she'd said. 'This is my father, this is my mother, and these are my brothers and sisters. And this is me.'

I found the photo at the very bottom of the drawer and took it to my room. It showed two young men, eight girls, a man with a white beard, and a woman whose braids were so long you could use them for jumping rope. A child on the left, a child on the right: *whoosh, whoosh, whoosh.*

The longer I looked at the photo, the more depth it acquired — the dreamy depth I'd seen in things as a child, as if I'd never really woken up, not quite. I saw a little girl smiling at me. She had shiny hair and a young, pretty face: my mother. She was wearing the uniform of Queen Victoria Girls Inter College. The two girls next to her were wearing the same clothes: dark dresses, white collars. They were the last two daughters to go to school, the youngest children. In the photo, their eyes sparkled like stars.

The girl to my mother's right was Sitara, a sister

whose son would one day fail to return from work —
one day, later, future and past.

Standing to my mother's left was Jasleen. She was
three years older and perhaps half a centimetre taller.
She was the only one not to stare into the camera
lens, as if her mind were elsewhere; as if she were a
dreamer, like me. Then the photographer released the
shutter: a flash, and a white cloud diffused.

Aunt Jasleen was an exceptional heptathlete. She was
the fastest of all eight sisters and was able to throw
the discus at least 40 steps, or if the person measuring
the distance had short legs, as much as 50. It wasn't
uncommon for the steps to be totted up by someone
who couldn't count very well. And so it happened that
Aunt Jasleen's training record stood at the magical
distance of 86 steps.

Jasleen Ahluwalia was unbeatable in the discus
circle. That's to say: she was unassailable if the wind
direction was favourable. Aunt Jasleen's talent only
manifested itself when there was a slight headwind,
which allowed the discus to climb higher and higher
before returning to earth after an endless descent. If
the wind came from the wrong direction — from the
back or sideways — or there was no wind at all, the
discus would slip out of her hand and tilt in the air
like a soup bowl before crashing down to earth after a
mere nine steps. It left everybody baffled.

These were India's immediate post-independence years. Athletics was still in its infancy. There were no clubs, no cinder tracks. The sport was played on hard, dry soil that wouldn't nurture grass. Cast-iron shots, javelins, discuses were a wondrous legacy from the British. What to do with them? Throw them — yes, but how?

My mother was highly skilled at shotput. Her secret: the use of both hands.

The trainers at Queen Victoria Girls Inter College were old, retired teachers who relied on unorthodox methods. Jasleen Ahluwalia was trained by a woman who swore by the use of chilli peppers: red peppers for the sprint events, green peppers for longer distances. Some peppers were so fiery they could blast an elephant a metre into the air.

Jasleen once finished first in the 1,000 metres, but kept running after crossing the finish line, making straight for the toilets. Success depended on the right dosage.

Every season there'd be a contest with another school, which would see the best pupils come out to defend the honour of Queen Victoria Girls Inter College. Jasleen was always selected for the heptathlon. Not only could she run fast and throw far, but she could also jump very high — by Indian standards, anyway.

The Fosbury Flop hadn't yet arrived on the high-jumping scene; it wouldn't be invented until years later, and adopted in India many years after that. The back-first jump by Richard Douglas Fosbury at the 1968 Olympic Games was imitated by Indian athletes from the word go, but the technique led to countless injuries: head injuries, broken bones, and even the occasional spinal cord injury. It was a kamikaze jump, the Fosbury Flop.

Jasleen swore by the scissors jump. She'd take a seven-step run-up and then quickly step over the cord, first with her right leg, followed immediately by her left. It was by far the safest technique, given that you landed on your feet. Behind the cord was no squashy mat, but a pit with sand and grit. The high jump and long jump were done in the same place.

My mother had developed a jumping technique that saw her use the pole to which the cord was attached. She'd take a run-up at a gentle 20-degree angle, grab the pole, push off and pull herself across the cord. Sometimes this would result in disqualification, but usually not. The fact that pole-vaulting wasn't a widely known event yet worked to her advantage. But I suspect she may have intimidated the officials as well. Being an official in India wasn't a sinecure. Some athletes simply pushed down the cord as they jumped: women who'd later drive their husbands to distraction, and who, at a young age, had already mastered the art of always being right.

The school record was held by Jasleen. It was a height that equalled the length of her mother's hair.

Every season, she'd add two centimetres, and in summer, even four, because her mother's hair grew faster at that time of year.

It was thanks to Jasleen's exceptional achievements that Queen Victoria Girls Inter College beat practically every other school in the vicinity. Jasleen got to mount the podium in every region, probably experiencing the same sweet afternoons I was to savour later. The setting sun, the thirst, and the satisfaction: these were glory days.

Like my mother, Jasleen was selected for the individual district championships in Lucknow. Thanks to her flying start, my mother won the large trophy that's now on her bedside cabinet. Jasleen won the heptathlon. The wind was just right, the peppers had been consumed in the correct dosage, and her mother's hair had undergone a growth spurt.

The winners in Lucknow went on to the championships of the state of Uttar Pradesh. This is where my mother made three false starts. It didn't stop her, though. She carried on sprinting and finished first, while the other athletes were still in the starting position. Never before had her headstart been this big. At the day's end, it took eight officials to pull my mother off the podium.

Jasleen, on the other hand, was allowed to mount the podium. Having set a new points record, she would be going to the championships in the north of India, in Delhi. At this competition, two months later, all the men's sprint events were won by Milkha Singh, The Flying Sikh. In Rome, in 1960, this prodigy would be the first Indian athlete to reach a final at the Olympic Games. He narrowly missed out on bronze in the 400 metres. But it was the closest an Indian athlete had ever come to winning a medal.

Jasleen won the heptathlon at the North Indian championships, and her name was plastered all over the papers. The press sang Jasleen's praises, as they'd done Milkha Singh's — with the same joy, the same big words: the nation's track-and-field hopes.

But unlike Milkha Singh, Jasleen would never compete in the Olympics. Her parents insisted that she go to university. Studying was higher in the Indian pecking order than sport. 'You'll reap the benefits of a university degree for the rest of your life,' her mother said. 'A trophy will get dusty and lose its lustre.'

Jasleen listened to her mother and became a lung specialist. The discus would never again shoot out of her hand and climb higher and higher on the wind before falling back down to earth, notching up innumerable steps.

I met the same fate. After my school exams, I was expected to become an economist, a lawyer, or a doctor. If I did, everything would be all right. I listened to my mother and went on to study economics at the Erasmus University Rotterdam. But I soon got bored, and drifted off in the recesses of the mind. I was never to wake again.

The day I announced my intention of becoming a writer, my mother burned a black bin bag out on the patio — just as she'd done for Mr Gerritsen, the tenant in the attic on Jericholaan. I could hear my mother yell: 'Be gone, spirit! Evil spirit of Ernest, be gone!'

She didn't want to see me ever again. She was ashamed of a writer, and still is.

But this is no revenge.

I'd love to hear her shout again — *'Jaldi! Jaldi!'* — and hear her voice ringing out across the grass, full of enthusiasm and jubilant happiness.

These days, I only hear it from afar, from the depths of a daydream.

THE DEATH OF GRANDMA
VOORST

We have Dutch relatives, too: Dutch aunts and uncles, grandpas and grandmas, nieces and nephews. The Van der Kwast family is characterised by bald men with moustaches, women without a sense of humour, and children with an interest in insects. The family doesn't boast a single drunkard, not a single artist, not a single poetic soul.

At one point, a certain Arie van der Kwast wasted his time drawing up a family tree, which can be admired online. Growing on it are names such as Eugenia, Johanna, and Helmerus, which bring to mind stern individuals who saw life as a duty. There was no such thing as pleasure, or else it was forbidden. Either way: the family tree contains not a single colourful person who took pleasure in life. No, none of that, please.

The family tree consists of a sturdy trunk, which

splits into neat, straight branches and a modest number of twigs. There's no uncontrolled growth anywhere and it's all blood and soil, from the root up to the crown. We're all made of the same stiff pale wood. Look at a Van der Kwast dancing, and you'll see a jumping jack puppet. Our hips won't budge.

And then my mother bursts in on the family, and the family tree starts swaying dangerously; the heavy suitcases, the broken radios, and the rusty bikes cause the old branches to moan and groan. Johannas down the ages call for an axe.

One of those Johannas is my great-grandmother, my father's grandmother. At the start of the twentieth century, she married a doctor. She was more than fifteen years his junior, still a girl, really. That's all I know about her biography. By the time I'm first deposited in her lap, she's well into her eighties. Her bones jab into my buttocks.

My brother and I call her Grandma Voorst, because she lives in Voorst, in an old people's home we've been visiting a lot lately. Since Grandma Voorst has grown demented, she's also grown milder.

As well as the hard bones, I remember Grandma Voorst's hair. I'd never seen such white hair in my life — whiter than the snow that fell from the sky in bucket loads during the majestic winter of 1985. We'd have to wait more than ten years for the next big white winter, but by then we'd almost stopped being children. You grow a little, and the world loses its magic.

We'd go to Voorst at least once a month, travelling the long distance in our first car, a red Lada with rust marks. Every now and then the exhaust would emit dark clouds and a couple of neighbours had to push-start the vehicle. My mother always egged them on in Hindi: *'Jaldi! Jaldi!'* When the engine finally started, my brothers and I had to jump in, and off we'd drive in our spluttering car.

On the way there, the three of us sat in the back seat, playing games such as 'I Spy with My Little Eye'. On the way back to Rotterdam, we'd each lie stretched out in a different part of the car: Johan on the floor, Ashirwad in the back seat, and me on the rear shelf. I remember the colours of the sky in summer — lemony yellow and fiery red, purple and dark blue — and the sound of the engine slowing as we exited the motorway. The sense of homecoming.

More often than not, the boot of the car was full of Grandma Voorst's things. My mother was keen to safeguard our inheritance; there were other interested parties. A visit to Grandma Voorst always began with a cross-examination.

My mother: 'Where's the cuckoo clock?'

Grandma Voorst: 'What cuckoo clock?'

My mother: 'There was a cuckoo clock on the wall.'

Grandma Voorst: 'What wall?'

My mother: 'Johan really liked that cuckoo clock.'

Grandma Voorst: 'Who's Johan?'

So then Johan had to come forwards and accept a pat on the head. I was always expected to come forwards when the family silver was at stake. My mother must have seen an economist in me quite early on.

The cross-examination was followed by tea and stale biscuits. As great-grandchildren, we were supposed to say how much we enjoyed visiting every month, while my mother would prowl around the house with a large bag in her hand, in search of items Grandma Voorst could do without.

Our biggest rival was my grandfather, Grandpa Luxembourg. That's what my mother thought, anyway. Once upon a time, my grandpa had left his wife for a young blonde woman with whom he then had three children in Remich, a small town somewhere on the Moselle. This second branch had caused a rift in the Van der Kwast family, breaking it into different camps that rarely saw each other. It was a miracle that the family tree hadn't split or toppled. Stiff wood, indeed.

Grandpa Luxembourg was great-grandmother's son. According to my mother, he'd changed Grandma Voorst's will when she'd already lost most of her faculties. During one of our visits, my mother demonstrated just how easily it was done.

'Grandma Voorst,' she said. 'Could you sign here, please?'

A sheet of paper was placed in front of her. Great-grandmother looked at it with her eyebrows raised. 'I can't read it. Where are my glasses?'

Her reading glasses were dangling around her neck, but my mother seemed to think there was no need for her to know this. 'You can sign right here,' she said, pointing to a place on the paper.

'What for?'

'For later,' my mother said, and smiled.

'Later is important,' Grandma Voorst mumbled, and put down a scribble.

My mother quickly pulled the piece of paper from her hands and said: 'You just signed a document saying we can remove your fitted kitchen.'

Grandma Voorst looked over at the door to the kitchen, a little disappointed, it seemed, but a minute later she'd already forgotten about the bequest. Throughout all of our visits, her attention was completely taken up by a raven on the balcony railing.

'There's my husband,' Grandma Voorst would say the second the black bird landed on her balcony. 'Hello, sweetheart.'

I'd reached the magic age at which I believed anything, but Johan refused to have the wool pulled over his eyes by the tall tales of grown-ups. 'That's a bird,' he'd say.

Grandma Voorst nodded. 'But inside that bird lives my late husband.'

Ashirwad pressed his face against the window and stared at the bird in disbelief.

'I spy with my little eye …' Johan said. 'A husband inside a bird!'

My mother tried to shed some light on the issue. 'Grandma Voorst's husband used to be a doctor,' she told us. 'He was really rich and owned a mansion in Laren. According to the terms of the will, that mansion will now come to Grandpa Luxembourg. In order to stop this, Grandma Voorst's late husband has returned in the form of a raven.'

This didn't make sense to either Ashirwad, Johan, or me.

'It's called reincarnation,' my mother said, and went on to explain that belief in this concept was perfectly normal in India, and that after death we all return, reborn in human or animal or plant form, depending on your karma. Either way, Grandma Voorst's husband had returned as a raven.

Ashirwad said: 'I don't want to come back as something else. I'm happy as Ashirwad.'

My father leaned over and whispered: 'I reckon it's time to go home. Why don't you say goodbye to Grandma Voorst?'

We lined up and pressed a kiss on great-grandmother's soft cheeks. Just about everything about Grandma Voorst was unappetising, but her cheeks were soft as velvet.

My mother had opened the door to the balcony and tried to lure the raven into the living room. 'Quick, Albrecht,' she said. 'Come in!'

Albrecht Johannes van der Kwast was my great-grandfather's full name. It's true that he'd been a doctor and that he and Grandma Voorst had lived in a massive house in Laren. He died long before I was born, at his desk in the study. A heart attack. It's a Van der Kwast death: without heroism, without applause; not in a theatre, but at home. Until recently, there'd been a painting of him in Grandma Voorst's bedroom. It showed a grumpy old man, with a bald head and a moustache, of course.

'Come, Albrecht,' my mother called out. 'You need to keep watch over everything!'

A moment later, we made our way to the Lada parked on the drive in front of the old people's home. And while the car whizzed across the road and the lavender sky slowly darkened, I sank into a dream on the rear shelf.

There was a lot of money at stake, especially when converted to rupees.

It was hard to imagine: Grandma Voorst was, if possible, even more frugal than my mother. When I reached school age and showed my great-grandmother my first report, she handed me a five-cent piece. 'Go buy yourself some ice-cream,' she said. 'Or French fries.'

I couldn't believe my eyes as I stared at the dark coin in the palm of my hand. My report boasted five 'excellents'.

Again, my mother tried to clarify matters. 'Grandma Voorst lived through the war,' she told us.

'At one point she was so hungry she had to eat flower bulbs.'

Ashirwad asked Grandma Voorst if flower bulbs were tasty.

It earned him a cuff around the ear. There were moments when Grandma Voorst still had a remarkably sharp mind. A couple of years later, Ashirwad might have dispatched great-grandmother to hospital, but now he sought solace with my mother. She whispered in his ear.

War and lifelong frugality — we knew the law of cause and effect all too well. Cause and disastrous effect. My mother had never eaten bulbs, but she'd been fed by a goat. Subsequent years hadn't seen much of an improvement. And now she never spent any money if she could help it, even though, like Grandma Voorst, she was practically a millionaire.

My mother and Grandma Voorst: they'd have made a good team. Both peed in the dark; both only ran the washing machine at night. They scraped clean every pot and pan after dinner, did the dishes with cold water, and never put the thermostat any higher than 18 degrees Celsius in winter. Unfortunately, Grandma Voorst wouldn't be around much longer. Just one school report, to be precise, but I wasn't to get any money for it — not even a cent.

With the dementia worsening, Grandma Voorst was forgetting more by the day: her food, her name, her underpants. The management at the old people's home had complained to Grandpa Luxembourg. They couldn't go on like this. One morning, Grandma Voorst had appeared naked on her balcony, shouting at the top of her lungs: 'Albrecht, come into my nest!'

Grandpa Luxembourg had his mother transferred to a nursing home in Oosterhout, in the province of Noord-Brabant. Here, Grandma Voorst would be lovingly looked after and there'd always be someone to help her with her underpants. My mother didn't agree with the decision. She didn't think very highly of geriatric care; love was in short supply in nursing homes. 'He's putting away his own mother,' she threw in my father's face. 'That way, he won't have to do anything himself. She'll die there, like a withered plant.'

Proceeding with extreme caution, my father began to list the advantages of a nursing home, but my mother wouldn't hear any of it. The last time she'd listened to my father was when she agreed to his marriage proposal.

'This is not how we treat family in India,' my mother shouted over him. 'We take older people into our homes and look after them. We treat them with respect, we don't put them into an extermination home.' It was the first time the term was mentioned. You might have thought it was a Freudian slip, but it wasn't. On all subsequent occasions, my mother also spoke of an extermination home.

In her view, Grandpa Luxembourg's decision was

prompted first and foremost by financial considerations. Insurance covered the costs: Grandma Voorst's bed and her incontinence pads, her food and drink. Besides, her new abode had no room for the things she had at the old people's home. Grandma Voorst shared a ward with three other corpses who were waiting for death to take the trouble to give them a peaceful grave. Her only possessions were a pink nightgown and a hairpin that kept her white hair together. The rest had gone to Luxembourg. It goes without saying that my mother wasn't best pleased with this. She'd screamed blue murder when the news reached her.

Apparently she'd forgotten Grandma Voorst's reaction when, a few years earlier, she'd been our guest on Tiberiaslaan. Since my mother was sorry that Grandma Voorst rarely left the old people's home, she'd invited her to spend the weekend in Rotterdam with us. It was a time when we were building enormous Lego spaceships, and our great-grandmother was still frequently lucid, although she had her absent-minded moments, too.

Since we didn't have a guest room, my mother had put a bed in the living room. Ashirwad had placed his cuddly toy on Grandma Voorst's pillow and sat down on the edge of her bed before turning in. Great-grandmother pressed my brother's stuffed monkey to her body and gave it a lingering kiss on the snout. It was a time when the toy didn't reek of a rugby club changing room.

'What's its name?'

'Teddy,' Ashirwad replied.

'But it's a monkey.'

Ashirwad nodded.

'Then why do you call it Teddy?'

'Because that's its name.'

For a split second, Grandma Voorst wondered if it was her, but then concluded that Ashirwad was the one who had a screw loose. 'You know what,' she said. 'I'm going to give you a pill tomorrow. In the old people's home, everybody takes them.'

Luckily, this was lost on Ashirwad. 'Sleep well, Grandma Voorst,' he said. 'Sleep well, Teddy.'

She kissed her great-grandson on the forehead and went to sleep with the cuddly toy beside her in bed. Grandma Voorst had survived this incident. But the following morning, not long after sunrise, we heard furious screams from the living room.

I was the first to reach Grandma Voorst's bed.

'Let me go,' she yelled. 'Let me out!'

I tried to calm her down, but got a pillow thrown in my face for my pains.

'Help!' Grandma Voorst yelled when my mother also appeared by her bedside. 'Another kidnapper!'

By the time we'd managed to convince Grandma Voorst that we were family, not kidnappers, we were well into the afternoon. The fact that we were keeping her from the phone probably didn't help. She wanted to contact the police and pass them the location where she was being held. We were looking at a prison sentence of at least ten years.

The sleepover had been hard on all of us, and so there was never a second visit. Perhaps a reminder of this weekend would cast a different light on Grandpa Luxembourg's decision to move Grandma Voorst into a nursing home, but my mother was a doom-monger when it came to family — especially when that family bore the name Van der Kwast.

A few days after Grandma Voorst was admitted, we went to visit the nursing home in Oosterhout. The red Lada had been replaced with a blue Peugeot, and although the car was bigger, I no longer fit on the rear shelf. My legs had grown too long. I would never again look at the world through the rear window of a car, or indeed through the eyes of a child. Time is cruel.

There was a funny smell in the nursing home. It got into your nostrils and even your clothes.

'It's the smell of death,' my mother said, oblivious to the two elderly people sitting in wheelchairs in the corridor.

At the reception desk, we were met by a lady with an unsmiling face. She'd crossed her arms.

'We're here for Grandma Voorst,' Ashirwad said.

Although our great-grandmother now lived in Oosterhout, we continued to refer to her as Grandma Voorst. Some things are slow to change. Besides, as we'd been told repeatedly during the 50-kilometre car journey, Oosterhout was a temporary abode.

'I have no Mrs Voorst on the register,' the woman said from behind the counter.

'That's not her real name,' my mother said.

'Her husband's inside a bird,' Ashirwad added, in the hope it would ring a bell. But the receptionist just raised her eyebrows and looked slightly alarmed.

Where we went, confusion soon followed. My father dealt with it by mentioning Grandma Voorst's first and last name. And so, a little later, we made our way to ward H2-13. But not before my mother had exclaimed: 'They can't even give us a smile in this extermination home!'

The receptionist didn't smile after this remark, either.

———

Grandma Voorst was muttering in her sleep: incomprehensible words aimed at the spirits haunting her final dreams.

Ashirwad wanted to shake her awake, but my father managed to stop him just in time. We had to wait for Grandma Voorst to wake up of her own accord. In the meantime, my mother rummaged through the drawers of her bedside cabinet, but found them empty.

'Nothing, nothing, nothing,' my mother lamented. 'Everything's in Luxembourg.'

As she said this, Grandma Voorst woke up with a loud scream. Her eyes took a while to get used to the light, but before long they fixed us with a hostility that seemed to originate in the war she'd lived through. The following moment, Grandma Voorst erupted in a tirade of obscene language.

We couldn't believe our ears. My parents regarded Grandma Voorst with pity, but my brothers and I saw a ghostly apparition. What time did to children was nothing compared to the havoc it wreaked on elderly people.

The screaming had attracted a nurse. He pushed Grandma Voorst down onto the bed and pulled out a syringe.

'A rat in Delhi has a better life,' my mother said.

She grew calmer. Grandma Voorst became Grandma Voorst again — except with trembling hands and tears in her eyes. A frightened animal. My father, her grandson, caressed her forehead. We took turns pressing kisses on her velvet cheeks. It was my mother who broke the silence with an Indian lullaby, a timeless lullaby. *'Chandaa maama door ke,'* she sang softly. *'Puye pakaayen boor ke. Aap khaayen thaali mein, munne ko den pyaali mein. Pyaali gayi toot, munnaa gayaa rooth …'*

Grandma Voorst returned to her dreams. How beautiful it would be, how mild and merciful, if we got to see the same at the end of life as at the beginning: the ancient, fabulous forests where there are more birds than tigers and more fruit than thorns, and where, in some dappled depth, the human spirit finally evaporates.

Our final visit took place three weeks before the end of the year. Johan and I sat in the back seat with our school report. Ashirwad had a drawing on his lap. He'd attacked a colouring picture of a butterfly with a red felt-tip pen. Colouring within the lines was another gift that hadn't been bestowed on him. But he was proud of his drawing and held it the way Johan and I held our reports.

A Christmas tree had been erected right by the door to the nursing home.

'A waste of money,' my mother commented, as we walked past the tree with tinsel. 'Most of them won't even make it to Christmas.'

This time Grandma Voorst was awake when we entered her room. She was sitting up in bed and even appeared to recognise us — as family, not as kidnappers. 'Theo,' she addressed my father. 'My little, bald-headed boy.'

My brothers and me were also given a warm welcome, except that Grandma Voorst got our names all mixed up. But that was nothing new.

My mother, however, didn't receive a greeting. Grandma Voorst simply didn't look at her.

We'd brought fruit: apples, bananas, oranges, and

a bunch of grapes. My mother had bought it at the market the previous day. 'At least she won't go hungry,' she'd said in the car. My mother was convinced that the nursing-home patients were deliberately starved, so nobody would last longer than a month. It's why she also left fruit for the other patients in Grandma Voorst's ward.

Ashirwad sat down on the bed and showed off his drawing. 'I made it for you.'

Grandma Voorst accepted the drawing gratefully.

'A butterfly,' Ashirwad said.

'Where?' Grandma Voorst asked.

'Right here.'

'That's not a butterfly, is it?' For a split second I thought Grandma Voorst was going to offer Ashirwad another pill, but instead her gaze hardened. She appeared to have seen something evil in the red lines my brother had scratched across the colouring picture.

My mother quickly lifted Ashirwad off the bed. He threw a fearful glance at his drawing.

Grandma Voorst began to scream — the same furious and obscene words as on our previous visit. But this time they seemed to be aimed at someone in particular … at my mother, to be precise.

'Calm down,' she tried to appease Grandma Voorst. 'Hush, now.'

She just ended up fuelling the flames. A series of explosive curses burst out of great-grandmother's mouth, most of which were unknown to me. I'd learnt to swear in Hindi.

And then Grandma Voorst shouted: 'Dirty tandoori face!' This was the climax of the series; the final beat of the drum. After that, all was quiet.

'She got that from Grandpa Luxembourg,' my mother whispered. 'The monster.'

We daren't breathe a word. Johan and I held our school reports with trembling hands — the beautiful reports we'd wanted to show Grandma Voorst, after which she'd give us five cents to buy ice-cream or French fries; five cents that our father would top up outside, as he always did, so we could *really* buy ice-cream or chips.

Grandma Voorst had screamed her lungs out. She was no longer sitting up, but lying down again. Yet neither Johan nor I thought this was the moment to present our school reports.

A nurse appeared in the doorway — a different one from last time, a new face.

My mother dismissed him, saying everything was fine. To our amazement, the nurse listened to her. He must have been a very perceptive man.

It lasted only a few minutes, the peace and quiet, the truce, and then Grandma Voorst slowly sat up straight again. She must have been looking for something, because her hands were fumbling along the underside of her bed.

'Can I help?' Johan asked tentatively.

'My axe,' Grandma Voorst muttered. 'Where's my axe?' And when she found nothing underneath her bed, she shouted angrily: 'Who stole my axe? Who was it?!'

The battle axe that had been buried by her deteriorating memory had miraculously found its way to the surface again. There was no stopping her now. 'Off with her head,' her 90-year-old lungs squeezed out of her body. 'Off with her head!'

In the bed opposite Grandma Voorst, an emaciated woman sat up, looked around, and began swearing as well. Up until this point, we hadn't heard a peep from the other patients on great-grandma's ward. If you didn't know any better, you'd have thought they were no longer with us. But now one of them started spewing out everything, all the filth, all the obscenity, she must have bottled up all this time.

It was surreal: two people with Tourette's in a single ward, playing a tennis match with genitals and other unmentionables. If I had to pinpoint a place I learned to swear in Dutch, it would be the nursing home in Oosterhout. The same is true for my brothers. Ashirwad is still reaping the forbidden fruits of it.

When the nurse finally returned, he didn't know who to sedate first.

My mother pointed to Grandma Voorst.

Three days later, she was dead. She didn't make it to Christmas. The news reached us from Remich. My father answered the phone, because my mother was in the kitchen. She had a rolling pin in her hand, which she tried to hurl over to Luxembourg seconds later, but which crashed into the floor lamp. Our household had acquired yet another broken object.

The funeral was in Laren, where Grandma Voorst would be reunited with her husband after three decades. The five of us travelled there in the blue Peugeot. It was a pale winter's day, with raw wind and black ice on the road.

We were quiet until we got to Gouda, when Ashirwad couldn't suppress his curiosity any longer: 'Will Grandma Voorst come back as a bird, too?'

'I'm afraid not,' my mother replied, and muttered something about her karma.

'What's she going to be, then?'

'I don't know.'

'How about a pig?' Ashirwad suggested.

'Maybe,' my mother replied. 'Maybe.'

'Or how about a rat in Delhi?'

My father pressed down hard on the accelerator, so we got pushed against the back seat for a moment and the Peugeot shuddered. Then the speed returned to normal, and we fell quiet again, all the way to the cemetery this time.

I remember the trees at the entrance to the cemetery: linden trees in winter. I remember our footsteps on the long, long path, with my cousins from Oudewater waiting at the end. They, too, had grown, but were still interested in the insect world and were now looking for larvae under the dead leaves on the ground. We looked at one another like strangers. Family: it didn't mean much.

Everybody was in attendance, except Grandma Ulft. Grandpa Luxembourg's ex-wife no longer showed up to the two occasions that brought the family together once in a blue moon: weddings and funerals. Her name was still included in the family tree, but that was it. Like my mother, she'd never forgive herself for marrying a Van der Kwast.

Uncle Herbert wasn't in attendance either, but then he never was. He was drifting through Canada, a backpack over his shoulders, a hipflask at his lips. The latest sign of life had been received quite a while ago.

Grandpa Luxembourg was there. He sat in the front row of the cemetery chapel. Sitting next to him was the blonde woman he'd married. The offspring from this second marriage had come along, too — aunts and uncles who were about the same age as me. They tapped one another on the shoulder, a game my brothers and I also played from time to time. Ashirwad always fell for it.

Having managed to escape my mother's watchful eye, I tiptoed to the front. After row upon row upon row, I suddenly found myself face to face with my grandad. He was bald and sported a moustache with ends that curled upwards. His eyes sparkled and he smiled at me. He didn't give me the surly look I'd seen in the painting in Grandma Voorst's bedroom, but a grandfatherly smile. 'You must be Ernest,' Grandpa Luxembourg said.

I nodded.

'Do you know who I am?'

I nodded again.

'Go on then, tell me.'

'The monster of Remich.'

The smile slipped from Grandpa Luxembourg's face.

'The monster of Remich who'd put his mother in an extermination home' was the full title my mother had bestowed on him. But my father didn't want me to say 'extermination home'.

When no response was forthcoming, I asked: 'How come the ends of your moustache point upwards?'

I'd never learn the answer, because my mother suddenly yanked me away. She dragged me to the back row, where my brothers were sitting next to my father. I wanted to whisper in Johan's ear, but a firm *'chup ho djao'* made me change my mind.

Everybody in the room fell silent. It was a strange silence, a silence I hadn't heard before — neither in the classroom, nor in the prayer room upstairs. I looked at the coffin on the platform. According to my mother, it was the cheapest one in the catalogue, a special offer. Ashirwad didn't believe it held Grandma Voorst.

Johan mumbled: 'I spy with my little eye ...'

'*Chup!*'

Some people dabbed their eyes with scrunched-up paper tissues, and my mother, too, shed a tear. We were too young for sadness; it didn't yet sting our cheeks. Grief was like a river that flowed past us.

A number of people — among them Grandpa Luxembourg — spoke about Grandma Voorst's life. But nobody said anything about her final days: about the balcony scene, the yelling, the harsh words. Nobody mentioned the timorous, trembling animal we'd seen. Death came with other stories, with kind words and memories of light.

Everything went well; everything was as peaceful as the footsteps shuffling towards the grave. Nobody had a go at one another with an axe or a rolling pin. Eternal peace descended on Grandma Voorst's coffin, along with large shovels full of dark soil. Tears were shed and flowers were laid, as they had been earlier in the morning for Mr Barendse, as they would be later in the day for Mrs Ending, and many others that week.

And perhaps everything would have remained just fine had Ashirwad not had a sneezing fit. The first sneeze lacked force, as though it were just a mistake, a mere displacement of air. But before long, the familiar explosions could be heard, and Ashirwad was showering the entire family.

I heard my father swear.

'It's not me who's doing it,' Ashirwad said to an aunt through marriage, who now had a string of snot dangling from her ear. 'It's doing it by itself.'

'Quick,' the aunt shrieked. 'A handkerchief, hurry.'

Taking advantage of the chaos, my mother walked over to Grandpa Luxembourg — right across the fresh grave. I saw her pull a piece of paper from her coat. She unfolded it and held it up to my grandfather. He looked at it with utter incredulity.

'The fitted kitchen,' my mother shouted. 'We get to have the fitted kitchen!'

Grandpa Luxembourg shook his head and was about to turn around when he was stopped cold. My mother's voice boomed across the cemetery: 'She signed!'

Death had finally granted Grandma Voorst a peaceful grave, but on top of that grave there wasn't much peace to speak of.

According to my cousins from Oudewater, Grandma Voorst wouldn't be fully consumed by maggots and worms until spring came around; only then would she be left in total peace. Forever.

I was hoping for a short, mild winter.

THE MAN WITH THE BEARD

Shortly after my mother arrived in the Netherlands, Uncle Herbert set off for Canada. A causal link seems obvious — an encounter, or a tin of cat food — but my parents didn't get to know each other until three years later, so all the signs are that Uncle Herbert emigrated quite by chance immediately after my mother's arrival.

Uncle Herbert's suitcases didn't contain bangles, necklaces, or earrings. No, he'd stuffed them with leaflets and old newspapers instead. The total came to about 40 kilos and was supposed to create the impression that he was an important man, someone with lots of assets.

Uncle Herbert was fleeing his home country, a milieu of narrowmindedness and floury potatoes. He'd left school at sixteen to train at agricultural school in Alkmaar, but never completed his course. Uncle Herbert had other plans — ambitious plans.

'Business,' he replied when the Canadian authorities

asked him about his reason for immigration. He showed the documents he'd obtained in the Netherlands: his passport, his work permit. Nobody asked him to open his suitcases; everything was fine.

Uncle Herbert had been to Canada the previous year. As part of an exchange programme at agricultural school, he'd worked on a farm in New Brunswick. There, Farmer Jake had introduced him to the language, the labour, the sweat, and last but not least, the dreams. Farmer Jake had bought a parcel of land, and with the proceeds of this land he was going to buy more land, and with the proceeds of that land, yet more land, even bigger and more extensive, on and on until he'd be rolling in it.

Six months: that's how long Uncle Herbert had stayed in New Brunswick. These months were to determine the rest of his life. Back in the Netherlands he felt confined, trapped by the system. He couldn't concentrate within the four walls of a classroom. He drifted off while listening to the lecturers' words, longing for the vastness of Canada, the land of endless opportunity.

Grandpa Luxembourg — not yet a grandpa at the time and based in Zutphen — was dead against his son's plans. Herbert was supposed to finish agricultural school and then go on to college in Bolsward. The family had no need for adventurers. Studying was the important thing; Herbert had no business outside a library.

Uncle Herbert didn't obey his father. One early morning in June, without a word, without so much as a wave, he disappeared. Two suitcases were missing, but that's all he appeared to have taken from home. A week later the waste-paper collector was given a disappointingly meagre stack, but nobody put two and two together and concluded that Herbert had taken the newspapers. Who would do such a thing? Who would cross the ocean with two suitcases full of waste paper?

Perhaps there's a Van der Kwast with a poetic soul after all. Uncle Herbert was bald and he had a moustache, but aside from that he was nothing like his kinsmen. He was unable to settle in the sodden clay soil of the Netherlands. In fact, he couldn't settle anywhere. His biography is full of gaps and holes, of vacant rooms and inhospitable plains.

My mother always worried that I'd take after Uncle Herbert and become a deadbeat, a vagabond, the black sheep of the family. And if truth be told, it's always been my secret wish to follow in Uncle Herbert's footsteps — big steps down long roads, taking me ever further from civilisation.

Business — that's the reason Uncle Herbert emigrated to Canada in 1969. He had no concrete plan, and didn't need one, either. There were plenty of opportunities. He'd assured his friends and classmates that he was going to be a millionaire, but they all just shook their heads. That's narrowmindedness and floury potatoes for you. But he didn't need their consent to become a millionaire. One day, you'd need a plane to see all of his land.

The first place where Uncle Herbert popped up was Petrolia, Lambton County, Ontario. It was a small town, with a population of 5,000, one high school, and five churches. More than a century earlier, James Miller Williams had struck oil here: a black jet from the earth that marked the beginning of the oil industry in North America. Fortune-seekers from around the continent overran Petrolia, digging and drilling all over the place. To this day, oil is pumped up from the same fields; the landscape home to a *perpetuum mobile* of pumpjacks.

Uncle Herbert put down his suitcases in front of the biggest office in town and knocked on the door. When a fat man answered, he held out his hand and introduced himself as Herbie. It's what Farmer Jake used to call him, and it's how he'd be known in Canada: Herbie van der Kwast, businessman.

He introduced himself, explained where he was from, and said that he'd heard Petrolia was in need of visionaries, entrepreneurs with grand ambitions.

'I'm your man,' Uncle Herbert said.

The fat man didn't react immediately. This was the first time in his life a bald man with a moustache had greeted him with the words, 'I'm your man.' He was reminded of an article in *The Petrolia Topic* about loose morals in Amsterdam. Without realising it, the fat man reached for the doorknob and explained that the only vacant position was that of a part-time secretary: three days a week.

Uncle Herbert thanked the man for his valuable time and picked up the suitcases with newspapers. He made his way to another office — less big, less lofty — but here, too, he found a man who looked more than a little surprised. Uncle Herbert didn't lose heart, picked up his suitcases again, and walked from office to office. But wherever he went, the story was the same. There was no business to be done in Petrolia.

Uncle Herbert was late — more than a century late. Perhaps he lacked my mother's powers of persuasion, or her rolling pin.

The only person prepared to give him work was a Presbyterian corn grower just beyond the city limits. It was harvest time. Uncle Herbert could start right away.

'I'm your man,' he said with enthusiasm. If a paperboy could become a millionaire, then why not a corn-picker? One day they'd be writing about him, about Herbie van der Kwast and his incredible career.

I'm writing the story now, because nobody else is doing it, because nobody else is familiar with it. To be honest, I don't know the whole story myself, all the details, all the facts, but that doesn't matter. It's the broad strokes that form the outline of a life. And it's the mind's eye that perceives things in this black void: a farm, a tractor, pylons on the land.

The farmer gave Uncle Herbert a small room in the attic and denim overalls with copper-coloured clasps and buttons. 'Strictly for workmen' it said on the label near his chest.

Uncle Herbert spent six days a week on a combine harvester, under the scorching sun, surrounded by acre upon acre of corn. When I close my eyes, I can picture him sitting there: happy and a long way away. On his own. It's as if my imagination is taking me by the hand, pulling me towards those golden fields: the rattling cylinder, a cloud of yellow splinters, and birds pecking the soil behind the combine harvester. They don't fly up as I walk across the mowed stalks. There's a sensation of freedom, of disappearing. When Uncle Herbert turns around, he looks at the trail he creates in the corn — a trail that will no longer be there at the close of day. I wave at him, but I'm invisible — that's the downside of fantasy.

On the seventh day, the church bells rang and Uncle Herbert was hauled out of bed. The farmer and his wife were going to the Sunday service, and he was expected to come along. In the wooden pews, he listened to a sermon about Jesus having shown the way, and man having to follow. The farmer and his wife nodded; Uncle Herbert bit his nails. The church reminded him of the classrooms in Alkmaar, prompting him to drift off on the preacher's words.

Three Sunday services later, the harvest was in. The land was now bare and darker in colour. The farmer moved differently, more calmly, and life moved indoors, where the machines were dismantled. Uncle Herbert learned the workings of an engine. These were days of oil and tar and heavy tools. The two men ended up with black hands and black faces. Their backs groaned.

When evening fell, Uncle Herbert would sit down under a tree, feeling exhausted, and look up at the sky. He taught himself to interpret the clouds, the sudden change in wind direction. He was now a man who could name engine parts and predict the weather.

Sundays were spent indoors: first in the wooden church pews, and then at people's homes. The farmer and his wife would introduce Uncle Herbert to other members of the community, people whose paths in life were as straight as the creases in their clothing. They were hoping he would meet a woman and build a life with her. They regarded him as their son, the child they were never able to have, which God had never given them.

Every Sabbath, they would go visiting in their Sunday best. Uncle Herbert drank tea and listened to the interminable clinking of teaspoons. He was usually placed between the farmer and his wife. In an armchair to the left sat the lady of the house, to her right her husband, and right across from him would be the daughter: a girl of barely 20 — sometimes extremely pretty, almost always ugly, with bushy eyebrows and the teeth of a horse. Few people, a closed community: inbreeding.

'Would anyone like another biscuit?' was a much-heard question from the lady of the house.

By the time a year had passed, the farmer made him a proposal with tears in his eyes. He wanted Uncle Herbert to become his partner, so he'd later be able to take over the business, including the land, the machines, the farm.

The farmer pointed to his golden land: all for his 'son'.

Uncle Herbert vanished the way he'd vanished from Zutphen — without a word, but with a suitcase in each hand. I can hear his footsteps in the night, in the blue morning. He's the only one on the road, a shadow underneath the stars. Here's a man who doesn't want to get married or have children. In the distance, light seeps into the day; in an hour's time, the farmer and his wife will wake up, waiting for the footsteps over their heads, the creaking of old floorboards. At a T-junction, Uncle Herbert puts down his suitcases in the sand by the side of the road. There are two directions, but whichever car stops will take him down the long road of the land of opportunity. I see him stare at the horizon, and moments later getting into a white pick-up truck. The wheels start turning, and the sand blows up.

The first gap in his biography is three months long. Perhaps Uncle Herbert is a would-be businessman in Hamilton, or maybe he leaves his suitcases at a motel in Markham, Peterborough, or Belleville, to spend his days in a factory making tornado sirens. It's monotonous work, all this clocking in and out.

Back home, in Zutphen, everybody was waiting for a letter, for a sign of life, nursing the quiet hope that one day he'd be back: their son, their brother, turning up on their doorstep, perhaps without a coat in winter.

The phone rang in the middle of the night. His voice sounded distant, as in a dream. 'Herbert,' Grandpa Luxembourg asked. 'Is that you?'

'I'm in Ottawa,' Uncle Herbert shouted. He was in a phone booth on Wellington Street, with cars whizzing past. It was evening, dinnertime, and people were rushing to get home. 'I found a job,' he said. 'I'm working in a laboratory.' Uncle Herbert explained that he'd been hired as a technical analyst at a dairy lab. He was doing research into lactobacteria. It was a full-time job, with a pay cheque every two weeks.

And then the connection was lost. The phone had swallowed all of Uncle Herbert's coins. Despite hearing nothing but noise from the underground cabling, the family held on to the receiver for a long time afterwards.

So he'd popped up as a technical analyst in a laboratory in Ottawa, nearly 600 kilometres northeast of Petrolia, as the crow flies. Wearing thick glasses and a long white coat, Uncle Herbert was using the knowledge he'd acquired at agricultural school to carry out experiments and tests. It was a life within the confines of four walls, but anonymous, without expectations, without any obligations. He could always pack his bags and leave. There was nothing that tied him to Ottawa.

He had no plants, no dog, no washing line.

One day, a colleague advised Uncle Herbert to invest in futures. Or did he get his information from a report in the local paper? Or maybe the hotdog seller on Elgin Street had mentioned it. Who knows — Uncle Herbert's sources were often dubious. He didn't go in for transparency; if so, anyone could become a millionaire.

And so it happened that Uncle Herbert invested all of his money in agricultural futures: wheat, corn, porkers, potatoes. Vast quantities of them; bushels, tens of thousands of kilos. It's a great business when prices are on the up. Within months, Uncle Herbert had amassed a small fortune. He used the profits to buy new futures, and in turn used their profits to invest in new, bigger futures.

Herbie van der Kwast, businessman.

He became a rich man — albeit very briefly. A mere flash.

And in that flash he bought houses and business premises, and he opened a large fishmonger's on 789 Somerset Street West. These days it's in Chinatown, and known as Ha Long Fish & Seafood Market, but once upon a time *'I'm Your Fish'* belonged to a bald man with a moustache. Wearing a green coat, Uncle Herbert sold fish freshly caught from the Ottawa River: carp, pike perch, eels, catfish. He worked from dawn to dusk and stank to high heaven. Never before had a Van der Kwast owned a fishmonger's, and never before had anyone in the family sold live eels, but perhaps a poetic soul is indispensable for this.

Uncle Herbert went bust almost overnight. The potato heralded his demise — not the floury Dutch variety, but the robust Canadian Hunter. A hundred thousand kilos of them, their price going into freefall. Corn followed, as did wheat. Only the porkers were turning a profit, but they could no longer save Uncle Herbert. He lost his houses and his business premises, his green coat and his fish. His sole possessions now were two suitcases. Taking them, he disappeared into the night.

The second gap is longer. These are years of silence, of isolation; rarefied air and footsteps in the snow. A cottage in Alberta comes to mind, in Swan Hills, Canmore, or Hinton — places along the edge of the wilderness, where temperatures dip below 40 degrees Celsius in winter. There, Uncle Herbert drinks steaming coffee from a mug. In the kitchen stands a woman, petite and with translucent skin. She keeps a diary, and is reserved in bed. She can't give herself fully; there's always some diffidence, some reticence.

They never fall asleep in each other's arms. In the morning, the woman wakes up before Uncle Herbert and tries to read his face, searching for salvation, for happiness in the lines around his mouth. But every day she sees the same: nothing.

In summer, Uncle Herbert repairs roofs, with his torso bared and a hammer in his hand. She teaches piano to children without an ear for music.

The woman is anticipating it, the day he'll leave. She knows it, has always known it. She knew it the day he entered her house with his suitcases. But she was willing to give it a try; you want to have faith. The same is true for Uncle Herbert; for anyone. We hold onto one another against our better judgement.

It takes years — six or seven long and harsh winters. Then spring arrives, and they let go of each other. They don't say a word; there's nothing to say. His footsteps on the wet path are the only sound. He follows the wind and vanishes.

The woman cleans the whole house, washing the sheets, the rugs, the curtains. She throws out the towels he used. In her diary she writes: *I hope this marks the beginning of my life.*

The gap is filled by a great-uncle: Willem van der Kwast — wooden hips, bald, moustache, the works. And yet he differed from the rest of the family in one respect. In every city he visited, he'd look for his last name in the telephone directory: in Groningen, in Leuven, in Hamburg, and in Vancouver, too. And so, during a business trip, he tracked down Herbert van der Kwast, isolated and alone on Canada's west coast.

The great-uncle ripped the page from the telephone directory and took a taxi to Herbert's house, an apartment on the second floor of a dilapidated building on Clyde Avenue, West Vancouver. Nobody answered, but the neighbour was so kind to talk to Willem van der Kwast from her window.

'Herbie's strange,' she shouted. 'He never says hello.'

He discovered three things: Uncle Herbert had no wife, he traded in penny stocks, and he smoked a pipe.

The great-uncle sat down on a bench opposite the house and waited until late at night, but Uncle Herbert never showed up. Maybe he'd spotted Willem on the bench and been shocked by the familiar figure.

'Maybe he's dead,' the neighbour in her nighty yelled before switching off the light.

Willem van der Kwast flew back to the Netherlands, taking the ripped-out telephone directory page with him, and shared his findings with the family.

'A pipe?' came the reply from Remich, from Rotterdam, and from Oudewater.

Nobody in the family smoked, and nobody in the family knew anyone who smoked a pipe. But Uncle Herbert had put an end to all that in one fell swoop. What other evolution would the Van der Kwast family live to see? Might Uncle Herbert's hips be molten, enabling him to dance like Elvis?

Several months later, my father managed to track down his brother in Vancouver. Ashirwad had already been born, while Johan was dreaming of birds and fruits in the womb. There was no sign of me yet. My mother was happy.

Uncle Herbert no longer lived in a dilapidated house, but on a dilapidated boat instead. The cabin had been fixed with tape and plastic carrier bags; the inside smelled of wet cardboard and mould. My father got to sit on the only chair. He explained that he'd been sent by the family. They were worried. Meanwhile Uncle Herbert prepared dinner: tinned kidney beans, heated over a gas burner. Simmering beans and the gentle swell of the water. Uncle Herbert was silent.

'Have you lived here long?' my father asked.

'About six months, more or less.'

'Will you be staying here?'

'No.'

A ship horn sounded, far off in the distance.

'The mooring fees are going up,' Uncle Herbert said. 'So I'll have to move soon.'

My father stared at the food rests in the corner of the cabin. This is what life looked like when its course couldn't be captured in three words: work, wife, child.

Uncle Herbert gave him the first tin, but its contents were still too hot to eat. My father waited for his brother to sit down opposite him, on the mattress he slept on at night. The two of them blew on their spoons.

'I was a millionaire,' Uncle Herbert said, between bites. 'And I lived with a woman who played the piano.'

'Mother misses you.'

'I'm better off on my own.'

'Where are you going after this?'

'Somewhere. Canada is a big country.'

'Won't you come back?'

Uncle Herbert got up and threw his tin into a corner. He pulled out his pipe. Filling it with tobacco took forever. When he was finally done, he said: 'What was that you asked?'

'Never mind,' my father replied. 'Forget it.'

The next day he travelled back to the Netherlands, to baby Ashirwad and my mother, to domestic life and the familiar Indian food.

'What's that I smell?' my mother asked at the table.

'Mmm,' my father said. 'Tandoori chicken.'

My mother shook her head. Although my father hadn't done any autopsies for over a week, my mother could still smell death. Pregnant women have a highly developed sense of smell. 'I smell corpses!' she said.

Uncle Herbert left Vancouver not long afterwards. The penny stocks had brought him to the brink of bankruptcy. The mooring fees had been raised, and a rental apartment was unaffordable. He was forced to seek his fortune elsewhere. Chance lent a helping hand.

On the day Uncle Herbert was due to leave Vancouver, he met an Austrian man who'd bought a marble quarry in Slocan Valley, more than 400 kilometres inland. He was planning to quarry the marble himself and sell it on the market. But he couldn't do so on his own. The Austrian man took a step back and looked Uncle Herbert up and down. 'You're my man!' he eventually said.

Uncle Herbert knew it: the suitcases, the 40 kilos of newspapers he'd been dragging along for a decade across half the continent, had finally done the trick.

And so he became a partner in a marble quarry he'd never even laid eyes on. The Austrian lifted the suitcases into the trunk and together they drove to Slocan Valley. It took them nine hours, traversing deserted highways, winding roads, and mud tracks right across Canada's unspoilt nature. The good news was that the marble was of the highest quality. The bad news was that the transport costs were too high to make the venture profitable.

'That's just like Uncle Herbert,' my mother would say later. When she finally met him, he still had the same talent: the talent to be in the right place at the wrong time; or in the wrong place at the right time; or quite simply in the wrong place at the wrong time.

Within six months, the marble quarry went bust. Uncle Herbert disappeared down a dark hole. Nobody knew where he was. He was everywhere and nowhere at the same time. Not a single telephone directory in Canada listed his name. Uncle Sharma had to haul himself through days of scorching heat and dust before his dream came true. Uncle Herbert wandered through an inhospitable landscape, through days of wind and ice, and more likely than not he'd abandoned his dream by now. He roamed across mountains and plains, land so vast you could only take it all in from a plane. He was the only person for miles and miles, but it wasn't his land. It belonged to the caribou, the chamois, and the bears; to solitude; and to the wind in the forest that slowly acquires a voice.

And then, completely out of the blue, he turned up on our doorstep on Jericholaan: a lean man with a beard and a black beanie on his head. My mother jumped out of her skin. She refused to let Uncle Herbert come in. 'Help,' she screamed. 'A tramp!'

'I'm Herbie.'

'I'm calling the police,' my mother yelled, the way Grandma Voorst had done when she'd mistaken us for kidnappers.

Uncle Herbert explained that he was my father's brother and that he'd come all the way from Canada.

'Impossible,' my mother said. 'Nobody in the family has a beard.'

True — a Van der Kwast didn't grow a beard. The moustache was our trademark; a beard was unthinkable, taboo even.

My mother wasn't having any of it, and so Uncle Herbert had to wait outside until my father came home from work. My brothers and I spent the whole day indoors. Our mother had told us that if we ventured out, we'd be robbed of our shoes.

From our position behind the first-floor windows, we watched the man with the beard. He had no suitcases with him; in fact, he didn't have anything with him. When Uncle Herbert spotted us, he waved. My mother quickly drew the curtains. 'Don't look,' she yelled. 'Don't look! It's bad for you.'

At six that evening, my father came home and walked into the living room with Uncle Herbert. We boys were expected to shake his hand, but none of us had the guts.

'This is your uncle from Canada,' my father said.

Then all three of us burst into tears. My mother came out of the kitchen and comforted us with the words: 'Don't be afraid. Uncle Herbert only *looks* like a tramp.'

He smelled of soil, of clay, and of something I couldn't immediately place, unlike my mother.

'What's that I smell?' she asked during dinner.

'Mmm,' Ashirwad said. 'Snakies.' His face was almost completely red. He sucked the strands into his mouth, sometimes ten at a time.

'What *is it* I smell?'

My father pressed his arms against his body and carried on eating as best he could.

'I smell garbage bags!' my mother said. 'The smell of garbage bags is spoiling my appetite.' She listed everything she could smell: banana skins, mouldy cheese, chicken bones.

I could smell it too, the smell of garbage. It emanated from Uncle Herbert, but it didn't seem to bother him in the slightest. He carried on eating. He had a huge appetite. My mother gave him three large helpings before confiding in me: 'Uncle Herbert is even poorer than a rat in Delhi.' My father whispered in my ear: 'But he's really happy, because he never married.'

After dinner, Uncle Herbert pulled out his pipe and filled it with tobacco.

'What's that?' Ashirwad asked.

'That's unhealthy,' my mother said. 'It turns your body black inside and then one day you drop dead.'

Uncle Herbert put the pipe in his mouth and got up from the table. He walked into the garden. Looking over my shoulder, I saw him standing on the grass. Small grey clouds escaped his mouth. They were smaller than those of Uncle Sharma — not winding lines, but little smudges, full stops, as if there was no story.

'It's something tramps do, too,' my mother said. 'Smoking, that is.'

Johan and Ashirwad would never touch a cigarette, cigar, or pipe in their life; they'd always steer well clear of smoking. In fact, Ashirwad can fly into a rage when you light a cigarette anywhere near him. Sometimes he'll suddenly start yelling to an innocent smoker at a bus stop: 'Go away! Otherwise I'll turn black inside!'

I'm the only one who has allowed the comfort of tobacco into his lungs, as well as the mysterious smoke of hash and marijuana. But it wasn't my thing, however desperate I was to belong with all those guys who refused to be trapped in the system, with the young men who viewed the world as their enemy, and who looked good in old clothes, in shabby coats and frayed trousers. I was too well-behaved, too much of a mama's boy.

Uncle Herbert stayed with us on Jericholaan for two nights before travelling on to Remich, to Grandpa Luxembourg. My mother gave Uncle Herbert a rolling pin to take along. She showed him how to use it as a bat. 'Raise it up in the air,' she explained. 'And then bring it down hard on his head.'

We'd never see Uncle Herbert again, but my mother reminded us of him often enough. Whenever we refused to brush our teeth, her voice would boom through the bathroom: 'You'll end up just like your Uncle Herbert!' The same would be yelled when we came home late, didn't eat fruit, or refused to go to bed. From a pedagogical standpoint, Uncle Herbert was valuable in the extreme: the kind of monster who'll always be scary.

When I got low marks in school, my mother came charging into my room, shouting: 'Your Uncle Herbert always had low marks, and he's come to nothing.' And later, when the first shadow of a beard appeared on my chin, she came after me with a razor: 'You'll end up in the street! You'll be begging just like him!'

At times it felt as if my mother's sole task in life was to keep us from turning into Uncle Herbert: a deadbeat, a vagrant with a black beanie. Her life's work could be destroyed by us fleeing across the Atlantic and entering the wilderness, just like Uncle Herbert.

The man with the beard is known to have popped up in two more places. The first location was Silverton, the tiniest hamlet in British Columbia, no more than a handful of houses along Highway 6. Keep driving and you don't miss a thing.

Uncle Herbert had stopped. He joined the voluntary fire brigade, which was never called out. On Tuesdays he worked as the local family doctor's clerk, and sometimes he helped out as ambulance driver. He lived with a woman called Judy, who had two children from a previous marriage. It was all explained in the missive that came through the letterbox years after his visit to us. It was a rectangular envelope with large stamps and a blue *Airmail* sticker.

At first, my mother kept the letter from us, but then she must have decided that the missive provided a valuable pedagogical lesson.

'This is what happens,' she shouted. 'This is what happens when you don't brush your teeth, your marks are low, you grow a beard, and you reek of banana skins. You end up in a little one-horse town with a divorced woman with two children.'

In my mother's eyes, there was nothing worse than divorce. It was one of the reasons she never warmed to Grandpa Luxembourg. But neighbours who split up weren't spared, either. We were no longer allowed to play with the children of divorced parents. If they turned up on our doorstep, my mother treated them to a sermon that ended with — you've guessed it — 'In India, nobody gets divorced!' Who knows, it may well be the reason why my parents are still together. Divorce is shameful.

'That's just like your Uncle Herbert,' my mother said, once she'd calmed down a little. 'In the wrong place at the wrong time.'

But Uncle Herbert wouldn't see out his life in Silverton. It was an intermediate station, like all places were intermediate stations for him. Sometimes he'd stay in a town a couple of days, sometimes several years. Estimates on how long he stayed with Judy varied. If she held him tight, the subsequent gap would be smaller. If her heart and her arms failed to get a grip on him, the gap would be a gaping chasm.

It was in this gap that we grew up. As Uncle Herbert drifted around Canada, I studied economics at Erasmus University Rotterdam, while Johan did research in Morocco as a physical geographer. For Ashirwad, time stood still. He sat in front of the window and looked out, at the world in which he'd never drive a car and never kiss a girl under a tree.

My mother sat by his side and answered his questions.

'Where's Johan? What's Ernest up to now?'

'Johan's doing research in Morocco and Ernest's studying to be an economist,' my mother explained proudly. This would be followed by: 'One day you'll go to university too.'

Her pride evaporated the moment Johan returned from Morocco with a beard and a car full of desert sand. Sitting next to him was a dazzlingly beautiful girl: long, dark hair, high cheekbones, emerald green eyes. A princess from the Sahara. He'd married her in a small village in Sehoul: a place of huts and sand; no-man's-land.

'Everything's been for nothing,' my mother wailed. 'Everything's been for nothing.'

The desert princess didn't receive a warm welcome. My mother went straight to the kitchen. The next moment Johan had a bump on his head. It was his first. There wouldn't be any roti on the menu for the foreseeable future.

There was only one thing worse than getting divorced, and that was marrying a Muslim. 'How could you?' my mother yelled at Johan. 'Muslims chased us out of our home and robbed us of all our

possessions. Girls had to cut their hair and wear boys'
clothes or they'd be raped. We had no food, no roof
over our heads!'

The last mouth had spoken — the mouth that had
been forced to drink the milk of a goat. *Pucha*.

With one hand Johan held his princess, while he
held the other pressed against the bump. 'Mum ...' he
said.

She shook her head.

'Mum,' my brother repeated.

'I'm not your mother anymore.'

Johan and his wife left. They drove out of
Tiberiaslaan with the engine screaming.

She was alone again, my mother — with her tears
and with Ashirwad.

A week later, I was the proud owner of a bump, too. It
turns out that a broken rolling pin is still an excellent
weapon. I'd come home because I'd run out of food in
my student digs, and because there was something I
wanted to tell my parents.

'I'm quitting my course,' I said over dinner. 'I'm
going to be a writer. My first book is coming out next
year.'

My mother slammed her fists on the table, sending
the plates flying. We were eating *penne* with tomato
sauce for a change — it must have been a special offer.
Ashirwad didn't like it much. Getting the penne into

his mouth was beyond him. The slippery little pasta tubes kept rolling off his fork.

'Effing tubes,' he muttered, as my mother ran into the kitchen. 'Bloody effing tubes.'

I failed to dodge the blow; in fact, perhaps I wanted that bump. Johan had one, so I had to have one too. It was the only way to break free from my mother.

'Everything's been for nothing,' my mother wailed again. 'I sacrificed my life for you. I was always home after school. I took you everywhere. I did everything for you.'

'I'm writing a book,' I replied, 'I'm not dying.'

But my mother didn't hear me. Her world had collapsed. My brother had married a Muslim woman, I wasn't going to finish my degree, and Ashirwad was Ashirwad and would always remain Ashirwad.

'I can't show my face anymore,' my mother sobbed. My father wanted to wrap his arms around her, but was swatted away. 'Keep your hands off me!'

My father quickly snatched the rolling pin off the table. He knew how to dodge blows; he was quite the expert in the field.

But there were other weapons. Before long, the first slipper whizzed through the air. My father ducked just in time. But the next one hit his nose. Slipper number two always hits the target. When a second later a metal trivet flew through the air, Ashirwad began throwing stuff, too. 'Effing tubes,' he shouted, as he hurled his plate across the table. My plate of pasta wasn't safe, either. My father's face was dripping with tomato sauce.

The bomb had exploded; our family was finished, just as the Polish poet Czesław Miłosz had prophesised.

'Uncle Herbert,' my mother sobbed. 'It's all Uncle Herbert's fault. He set a bad example. Now Johan has a beard and Ernest's packing in his studies. My whole life has been for nothing.'

I shook my head. Uncle Herbert had shown me the way — not the straight, direct way, but the winding path through the wilderness. 'I don't want to be like everyone else,' I shouted. 'I want to roam around, I want to smell of banana skins, and I want to be penniless!'

That same evening my mother burnt a rubbish bag on the patio. 'Be gone, spirit!' she screeched. 'Evil spirit of Ernest, be gone.'

I never disappeared. I'm still sitting here at my computer. I stare at my screen, picturing things that aren't there: the bluish haze, the longing to be elsewhere. But I'm inside and not outside, not in the big wide world. My life could be summed up in three words: work, wife, child.

After many, many years, Uncle Herbert popped up in Alberta. He was now working on the Athabasca Oil Sands. Oil-sand mining: work made near impossible in summer by the mud and the mosquitoes, while in winter the earth froze so vehicles could barely reach the remote mines. Uncle Herbert sat on a shovel, digging up the black oil-sand fields. Cold hands, cold feet, cold bones. Some weeks he worked nights, when everything was dark, save for the headlights of giant lorries coming and going.

Did he think of his days in Ontario? Did his imagination pull him back to the golden fields of Petrolia, where he sat atop a combine harvester? Or did he think of a girl sitting opposite him in a living room full of clinking teaspoons? Ensconced in the cabin of that shovel, did he long for a home?

This is where the trail ends. Uncle Herbert's last letter was posted in Fort McMurray, the only town in the Athabasca Oil Sands. Grandpa Luxembourg received the envelope with the red maple leaf. *Oil sand kills the soul*, Uncle Herbert wrote. He'd handed in his notice; he couldn't hack it anymore. *I don't know where I'm headed next. The north appeals to me: the Northwest Territories, Yukon, Alaska. Plenty of opportunity.*

I can picture him walking down solitary roads. He has no suitcases in his hands; he doesn't look like an important person. He's a nobody. Perhaps a logger gives him a ride, or perhaps he spends three days on a bus and gets off in another province. There's always work to be had in the wilderness. First-aid posts need to be manned in winter: for six consecutive weeks, with satellite phone the only contact.

There's an aid post in the west of Yukon. It's a

former US air-force base, with low buildings dotted around a barren plain, caved-in hangars, hundreds of aeroplanes, and tanks rusting away. Uncle Herbert peers through binoculars at the vast emptiness; this is bear territory, but he hasn't seen any yet. It's so cold he has to keep the diesel engine of his car running day and night to prevent the oil from clotting.

There's only the occasional callout: hunters, trappers, Inuit needing assistance. The rest of the time, Uncle Herbert is on his own. He sleeps on a camp bed and warms himself by an open fire. He tries to predict the weather. Sometimes he works a double shift: two-and-a-half months of severe frost. His provisions are dropped from a plane — the plane that overlooks the vast country.

He's a lonesome cowboy without a hat, without a horse, without cattle. He's a cowboy in the wrong place, on a prairie of frozen marshland.

'Just like your Uncle Herbert,' my mother would say.

At first she didn't want to emigrate to Canada, terrified as she was of bumping into Uncle Herbert.

'We're going to Toronto,' my father said. 'Herbert's on the other side of the country.'

But this didn't quite put her mind at rest. To this day, she's worried a man with a beard and a beanie on his head will turn up on their doorstep, swathed in the smell of a rubbish tip. That's family for you.

I don't think Uncle Herbert will pop up again. In summer he probably lives in a trailer on some farmer's land. He doesn't talk much and grows his own vegetables. These are days of tall grass and blue skies. The winters he spends up north, on his own for weeks at a time. I can see him walking, a backpack over his shoulders, a hipflask at his lips. I can hear his footsteps — *clomp, clomp, clomp* — removing themselves ever further.

Imagination gives birth to the dream. But I don't follow in his footsteps. I don't dare. I don't have a poetic soul, either.

Clomp, clomp, clomp.

Then all goes quiet. Even in the land of boundless opportunity, a man can disappear.

IN INDIA

DELHI, it says on the screen above the check-in desk.
Queuing in front of me is an Indian family: father,
mother, four children, eighteen suitcases. When it's
their turn, the stewardess takes a deep breath. The
father lifts the first suitcase onto the luggage belt. Its
weight is displayed: 32.4 kilos.

'Too heavy,' I hear the stewardess say. Not long
ago, the allowances were reduced to no more than
20 kilos per person.

A discussion ensues. The mother does the talking.
She points to her four children and then at the
enormous suitcase on the luggage belt. The stewardess
fails to see the connection. The mother tries to remain
calm, but when she sees the head shaking behind the
desk, she loses her patience and starts swearing.

The stewardess refuses to budge.

The father takes the suitcase off the luggage belt.
His wife points to another suitcase. This one is also

too heavy. Again, the digits pass a fatal judgement.

A rearrangement follows. All the suitcases are opened, and hold luggage is transferred to hand luggage and vice versa. Some things end up in the father's pockets. He stuffs toys and food into his coat.

The man reminds me of my own father, who was always sent through security with a heavily weighed-down coat. My mother forced him to smuggle any excess weight in his pockets. Usually it went well, but on the odd occasion he'd be searched and made to hand over 20 pounds of chocolate or remove a saucepan from his inside coat pocket.

My mother: 'I told you to comb your hair!'

My father: 'I have no hair.'

'What's this, then?' My mother pulled at the sparse grey tufts above his ears. This was her theory: with uncombed hair, my father looked like a criminal on the run and was likely to catch the attention of security officials. According to my father, it was all down to the way in which he staggered through the security gates with the excess weight in his coat.

The Indian father heaves the enormous suitcase back onto the luggage belt. This time it weighs just over 28 kilos — still too much.

The stewardess explains that she has to charge them 100 euros for every five kilos of excess weight. The mother yanks the suitcase off the belt and calls the stewardess the daughter of a South-Indian beggar woman.

Indians don't pay for excess baggage.

A Netherlands-based relative — a cousin or an uncle — is called over. Dozens of things are pressed into his hands. This reorganisation takes forever as well. The Indian family's children are sitting on the floor, playing. They've clearly seen it all before. It was the same in our family in the old days. We often had enough time to play a whole game of Ludo while queuing for the check-in desk.

Finally, they arrive at the correct weight. The stewardess labels twelve suitcases, and one by one they travel down the luggage belt and into the belly of the airport. The other suitcases can be taken on board as hand luggage.

'*Jaldi*,' the mother tells her children. '*Jaldi! Jaldi!*'

Then it's my turn. I'm carrying two pieces of luggage, two suitcases. My heart starts beating a little faster as I place my hold baggage on the belt. The display indicates 17.7 kilos. It gets the seal of approval.

'Passport?' the stewardess asks.

I pull my passport from my travel wallet and put it on the desk.

The stewardess leafs through it and says: 'You have no visa.'

'Do I need one?' is the first thing that comes to mind.

'Yes.' A single word, no more.

'But I was born in India,' I say. 'In Mumbai.'

The stewardess smiles. The corners of her mouth curl up a little, and there are creases around her eyes.

I'm ashamed of my answer: a half-Indian who thinks he can enter the country without a visa.

'I'm afraid we can't let you board,' the stewardess says.

'Can I not get a visa at the airport?'

'You'll need to go to the Indian embassy in The Hague for that.'

A torrent of abuse wells up — ten different Indian words for 'promiscuous woman'. But I meekly take my suitcase off the luggage belt. The digits jump back to 0.0 kilos.

'You can change your ticket in Departures Hall 1.'

I step out of the queue and make my way to customer service in Departures 1. The re-booking fees are exorbitant. My mother would have yelled that in India you can buy an entire plane for that sort of money. I pull my credit card through the machine before beating my retreat to The Hague.

The Indian embassy is closed, but I can go to India Visa Services, an intermediary. An employee hands me an application form and asks me to fill it in at one of the tables. 'If all goes well,' she says, 'your visa will be ready tomorrow.'

I answer the questions on the form and hand it back. The assistant shakes her head. 'This is going to take weeks,' she says, pointing to the line where I wrote down my profession: *writer*.

I'm handed another application form. 'Accountant, electrician, waiter,' the assistant says. 'Anything's better than a writer.'

'I was born in India,' I'm tempted to say. 'Surely I'm allowed to visit my family!' But I know there's no point, and swallow my words. At the table, I fill in my data for the second time: name, address, passport number, place of birth, nationality. Then I get to the line where I'm supposed to fill in my profession. I think of my mother, of my mother's dream, of the dream none of her children fulfilled — neither Ashirwad, nor Johan, nor me. My hand trembles when I write on the dotted line what I never became: *doctor*.

This time the India Visa Services employee nods her approval. 'You can collect your visa tomorrow, late afternoon.'

Two days later I fly to Delhi, back to the country where I was born and where I haven't been for more than 20 years.

The Indira Gandhi International Airport smells of my mother's kitchen: onions, spices, red chilli peppers. It's warm and crowded. I wheel my suitcases through a line of men with signs around their necks. One of those men is Uncle Kakar, the husband of Auntie Sitara, the third youngest daughter after my mother and Aunt Jasleen.

'Do you remember me?' I asked Auntie Sitara when I phoned her from the Netherlands.

After a moment's pause, she said, 'Yes ... You were small and very naughty!'

My memories of my last visit to India consist of little more than clouds of smoke. But that was in Bombay, with Uncle Sharma. We also visited Noida, where the Kakar family lived.

I told Auntie Sitara that I was planning to travel to India to visit relatives. 'You're very welcome,' was the immediate reply from the other end of the line. 'Family is always very welcome.'

So now I'm wheeling two suitcases through Delhi airport, in search of relatives I don't remember. I cast my eyes over the many signs with names on them before spotting *Doctor Ernest*. The sign hangs around the neck of a short, slim man.

'Uncle?' I say.

The man smiles.

We shake hands, but don't know what to say. 'Come along,' my uncle says after a while. I follow him to the exit. He keeps the sign with *Doctor Ernest* around his neck. Some people eye me with curiosity. Outside, we're given priority at the taxi rank.

It takes about an hour to get to Noida. On the motorway, Uncle Kakar asks if I had a pleasant journey. He still hasn't taken the sign off, which has me slightly worried that my mother told him that back home I'm a famous dermatologist or something.

She'd be proud enough to do so. Then it turns out that I owe my title to my economics degree — a degree I supposedly completed, and with distinction, too.

'And now you're a writer,' Uncle Kakar remarks. I hear surprise in his voice, as if he can't get his head around this progression from doctor to writer. He mumbles something in Hindi, the mother tongue I never learned.

It's dark, close on midnight. I look outside, trying to catch a glimpse of the country of my birth. Dozens of men with brushes in their hands line the road. They're covering the concrete step barrier in black and white stripes. Without slowing down, we whizz past the painters. Further along, traffic is held up. A man lies on the road. We drive past the accident at a crawl. It's plain to see that a car has driven over the man's head. His skull is dented, squeezed, it seems. It's my first impression of India, and suddenly I'm overcome with fear — of the country, the people I don't know, and the language I don't speak. What am I doing here? What am I hoping to find?

Auntie Sitara opens the door in her nightgown. She hugs me a little awkwardly. 'You've grown so big. You were so little back then ...' she says. *'Tutto baby.'* She laughs at her own joke.

We make our way to the kitchen. Uncle Kakar gestures for me to sit down at the table. The sign is still around his neck. Perhaps he has forgotten he's wearing it. Or maybe he'll be wearing it for the duration of my stay, like I had to wear my medals for a week. It allowed everybody to see I'd won a prize — neighbours, teachers, even the cashiers at Den Toom supermarket.

My aunt asks if she can get me something to eat. Again, she flashes me her warm smile, but there's sleep in her eyes.

I thank her, and tell her I'm not hungry.

'Anything else?'

'*Pani*,' I say, to make things easy for her. *Water* — one of the few innocuous Indian words I know. My mother must have taught it to me when I was still small.

I'm staying in a room with a narrow bed and a fan, which my uncle demonstrates with the fervour of a salesman. 'It comes with a remote control,' he explains. 'It has three different settings.' I look up at the rotating ventilator above my head, and see the blades turn faster and faster. 'Feel free to leave it on all night.'

At some point my aunt intervenes and remarks that I must be tired. 'Good night,' she whispers before closing the door behind her. Sleep comes fast — a wave that immerses me in a sea of dreams.

The following morning, I find my aunt and uncle in the living room. They're still in their nightwear and doing relaxation exercises on the floor. Their eyes are closed and the television is on. Images of a priest singing into a microphone are interspersed with shots of gilt roofs.

I sit down on the couch and look at my mother's sister. While taking a deep breath, she lifts her arms above her head. I try to identify the features she shares with my mother. But Auntie Sitara looks like my mother the way all Indian women look like her: petite, with long, dark hair, and skin the colour of milk chocolate. If you told me Auntie was a stranger, I'd believe you, too.

A little later, we're sitting at the kitchen table. I'm given toast, while my aunt and uncle eat rotis with vegetables. They're dressed now, and luckily my uncle is no longer wearing the sign around his neck. Auntie asks if I slept well. Again, that smile, and then suddenly I see it: the resemblance. She has the same straight white teeth as my mother. Slowly, I begin to see more similarities: the dark spots under her eyes, the down on her cheeks, the tiny wrinkles above her nose. It's as if my mother's face is buried within hers. Yet at the same time, Auntie Sitara is totally different. I attribute it to the peace, the harmony. Uncle doesn't keep his arms pressed tightly against his body; he eats his breakfast calmly. In this household, the rolling pin is only used in the kitchen.

As I take a sip of tea, I notice the ABN AMRO bank logo on my mug. 'The last time your mother came to visit, she brought lots of gifts from the Netherlands,' Auntie Sitara says. She points all over the place. I follow her finger and see an ABN AMRO clock, an ABN AMRO lamp, and an ABN AMRO digital thermometer.

I can't believe I didn't notice any of them last night.

'And that's not even the half of it,' my uncle says.

I nod. I can imagine. My mother may well have around 20 ABN AMRO accounts. I remember many a visit to the bank as a child. If you opened a new account, you'd receive a set of pens, or perhaps an electric flyswatter. These promotions were meant to attract new customers, but my mother had found a loophole in the system. She'd simply get cash out of the machine outside and deposit it into a new account inside. Free is good. And so we went home with gadget after gadget, as if we didn't have enough junk already.

And now my aunt and uncle are saddled with all this stuff. They seem fine with it, though. Perhaps my mother told them that ABN AMRO is a well-known designer brand.

'We've got chocolate wafers, too,' Auntie Sitara tells me.

In the afternoon, I go for a walk. Noida is a relatively new town just outside Delhi. Most people living here are well-to-do. Cars are driven by chauffeurs, while guards can be seen dozing on chairs outside some houses. In small huts, laundry is ironed with coal-filled irons. I walk down roads made not of dirt but of asphalt. Rickshaw cyclists offer to take me places. Cows graze amid the honking traffic. When schoolchildren in uniform wave at me, I wave back, eliciting loud laughter. I'm the stranger here, not them. Close by, women with large bags stand in front of vegetable stands. They're haggling.

Upon my return, I find my aunt outside on her balcony. 'Where were you?' she yells down. 'I was so worried.'

She hugs me when I'm by her side. 'Everything's fine,' I say. 'I just went for a walk in the sunshine.'

It's a while before her arms let go of me. Auntie goes over to the kitchen and boils some water. We drink tea at the dinner table. She drinks her tea with milk, me without. Uncle is in bed, taking a nap.

'I usually take an afternoon nap as well,' my aunt tells me. 'But I was so worried.' Her eyes fill with tears — a sea to the left, a sea to the right. 'One day our son didn't come home,' she explains. 'He got hit by a drunk driver on his way back from work.' I know the story; my mother told me. He was the same age I am now: 28.

Auntie has my mother's eyes, too — the same dark pools of sorrow. But I also see peace, inner calm instead of undying hope.

Snoring can be heard from the bedroom. 'Uncle snores louder than all the Ahluwalias put together,' Auntie Sitara says and laughs again. Then she goes for a lie-down.

I try to write in my room — the beginning of this story. I can't do it; it's too early still. I've no idea where it's headed. It's set in India, but then what? The fan whirs above my head. *Whoosh, whoosh, whoosh*. But nothing happens.

Maybe I need to get used to the calm. There are no slippers flying through the air, no neighbours being poisoned. Auntie Sitara is the milder version of my mother. She talks calmly and cooks without chilli peppers. She loves her husband. At night, she sits down on the end of my bed and talks about the role of spirituality in her life. Every morning she rises at four to meditate for two hours. This is followed by a walk with her husband and relaxation exercises together. And so, they grow older and older and older.

I tell her that my mother is quite different. Auntie laughs. 'Wait till you meet Aunt Jasleen,' she says.

Jasleen Ahluwalia, the fastest of all eight sisters, and once unbeatable in the discus circle.

'Sometimes we hide when she comes to visit.'

A couple of days later, the phone rings. It's Aunt Jasleen. The first thing she asks is why I haven't been to visit her yet. I don't get a chance to respond. 'You must come and visit me immediately,' she says.

Within less than an hour, she turns up on our doorstep. She's just as short as my mother and Auntie Sitara, but her hair is grey. She doesn't dye it. She has more wrinkles, too.

I feel as if I'm being kidnapped. I just manage to pack a few items — my toothbrush, my laptop, a book

— before Aunt Jasleen drags me to the kitchen, rolling suitcase and all. She never lets go of my wrist.

Her sister is preparing rotis for me. 'For the journey,' she says, since I haven't had any lunch yet.

'Do you think he won't get any food at mine?' Jasleen shouts. 'Do you think I'll let him starve to death?'

Uncle quickly slips to the bathroom, where he locks himself in.

Auntie Sitara is holding a rolling pin in her hand, but doesn't use it to attack her sister. Calmly, she rolls out the dough and bakes three rotis in a cast-iron pan. She breaks off a small piece of the last roti. 'Three is unlucky,' she says, and smiles.

'Come,' Aunt Jasleen barks, and drags me outside, where a yellow Toyota is waiting. She gets in and slams the door shut.

I turn to Auntie Sitara, who has followed us to the car. She reaches out and hugs me. 'Come back in one piece,' she whispers in my ear. *'Mera baccha.'*

A long time ago, my mother used to say *'mera baccha'* to me: my child.

As we pull away, Uncle comes out of the house. He and his wife wave goodbye. Aunt Jasleen growls like a tiger warning its prey. Next time, you're dead meat.

I lean against the back rest and try to relax. *She's family*, I tell myself. *You're in good hands.*

'This is my chauffeur,' says Aunt Jasleen, and points to the boy sitting next to her. 'I'm giving him driving lessons.'

The kid smiles at me in the rear-view mirror. He can't be much over sixteen.

'He's very talented,' Aunt Jasleen says, as I try to locate the seatbelt, which must be tucked away somewhere underneath the back seat. 'I found him in the street. He used to work as a shoeshine boy. Now he's my chauffeur.'

When I finally discover a seatbelt, it's stuck.

'Indicator,' my aunt tells the kid. And to me: 'He keeps forgetting his indicator.'

Like a man possessed, I tug at the seatbelt. It won't budge, not a centimetre.

Meanwhile, my aunt issues another instruction. In Hindi, so I don't understand what she's saying. Maybe it's along the lines of: 'Gently release the clutch.'

My father gave me my first driving lessons on a deserted industrial estate. I drove up and down a wide road at 30 kilometres per hour. There wasn't a soul in sight. But this is India. There are five rows of cars on a two-lane motorway, and among them are trucks, overcrowded buses, tractors, bicycles with washing machines on their pannier racks, bicycles with water tanks, and bicycles with poultry, regular rickshaws, motorised rickshaws, beggars, cows, camels, and goats. There's even the odd elephant. And everywhere you look, women and children are crossing the road. And everybody honks — not just once, but non-stop. The first thing an Indian does when he buys a car is try out the horn. *Honk! Honk! Honk!*

'Brake,' my aunt yells.

My body slams forwards and I hit my forehead against the headrest in front of me. The next moment, my aunt bursts into a tirade I can follow word for word. I'm not sure who she's targeting, though: the boy she's teaching to drive, the car in front of us, or the car to our left? All the cars around us?

I think about the three rotis minus the one pinch I'm carrying with me, which are meant to ward off bad luck. I hope they'll do the job. 'Is it much further?' I ask.

'We're nearly there,' Aunt Jasleen replies. 'But we've got the traffic against us.'

Eventually, we make it to Ghaziabad in once piece. Like Noida, it's close to Delhi. We drive around a modern neighbourhood. Aunt Jasleen proudly points to the houses: 'It's all doctors around here.' We stop in front of a white villa, but don't get out of the car. I'm told to take a picture. 'So you can show everybody back home what kind of neighbourhood I live in,' Aunt Jasleen says.

I take my camera out of my suitcase and on my aunt's instructions shoot a series of photos of the façade.

Then we drive to another neighbourhood. The houses are less modern here, but still big. On bits of undeveloped land, people have erected tents of cloth and cook over open fires. I see naked children running across the loose sand.

The car comes to a standstill in front of a house that's still under construction. The upper floor is covered in scaffolding.

'Here's where I live,' Aunt Jasleen says.

We get out and walk to the front gate. Behind it, a dog is jumping up and down. My aunt opens the gate and starts petting the animal. 'Mittu,' she sings. 'Oh, my Mittu.' The dog rubs up against her legs.

I'm told to take another picture — not of her and the dog, but of the sign on the façade. It boasts a red cross and below it, in hand-painted letters: *Doctor Jasleen Ahluwalia.*

'Did you get a good shot?' she asks.

I show her the result on the camera's LCD screen. Aunt Jasleen dons her reading glasses and exclaims: 'My house! My sign!'

Inside, I'm given an extensive tour. Her practice is based on the ground floor. There's a waiting room and a consulting room. A stethoscope on the desk is covered in a thick layer of dust. Likewise, the chairs are covered in grit.

'I'm retired,' Aunt Jasleen explains. 'And the cleaning lady ran off.'

Her pride and joy is the separate entrance. Together we walk down the corridor that her patients used to walk through to see her. I'm a visitor to a museum that's opening its doors one last time. My footsteps leave a trail in the dust on the flagstones.

The residential part of the house, one floor up,

smells of food. The rooms are spacious, the furniture is sparse; some rooms are empty.

'I have a huge house,' my aunt says. In her eyes I recognise my mother's gaze, as she looks out across Lake Ontario.

There's another floor, but it was never completed. There's no glass in the windows, and the walls haven't been plastered yet. There are bags of cement everywhere.

Aunt Jasleen opens a cupboard full of tools. 'I confiscated all of these,' she says. 'That should teach them!'

I nod. I can imagine — imagine something terrible, that is. I think about my mother's many conflicts with workmen. On completion she'd always find a fault, or some other problem caused by the work done. I remember Theo, who worked cash-in-hand and built us a second bathroom on the upper floor of the house on Tiberiaslaan. When the bathroom was done, we had a leak in the living room.

'It's raining,' Ashirwad said when Johan was having a shower on the floor above.

As my mother mopped the floor, she told herself off. 'I should have known,' she muttered. 'His name's *Theo.*'

The following day the leak was repaired, but the cash-in-hand man could kiss goodbye to his money.

'Water damage,' my mother said, pointing to the stack of VCRs. 'All broken.'

Theo looked at the VCRs. 'Weren't those defective already?' he asked.

'I could have made countless Indian families happy with those VCRs,' she yelled. Then she went to the kitchen and chased the cash-in-hand man out of the house in the time-honoured way.

In the end it was my father who secretly handed Theo his wages, in the same way he paid most handymen. He was constantly intervening between my mother and painters, plumbers, carpenters, and builders — sometimes all the way to court. It must have cost him hours and hours' worth of prostate cancer research.

Aunt Jasleen has to do it all without my father, without mediation, without secret payments. She does everything with her pride — pride cast in concrete. She won't yield to the builder who rips her off or cheats her in any other way. Her beautiful house will never be completed.

After the tour, we drink tea in the living room. Aunt Jasleen wants to know: 'Where's it better? Here or with Auntie Sitara?' Luckily she supplies the answer herself: 'It's much better here. You're practically living like a maharaja.' Her eyes are beaming. She's come a long way, as long a way as my mother.

Tentatively, I ask her about the past, the dark cloud over their history.

'Is it for your book?' Aunt Jasleen asks.

'Maybe.'

'Your mother's furious. She's losing sleep over it. She claims you're ridiculing her in your book.'

'It's fiction.'

Aunt Jasleen looks at me long and hard before saying: 'If you write about me, I'll kill you.'

I nod. I know what's in store for me. It's not everlasting glory.

My aunt starts talking. The beginning is pure slapstick. My mother's father's father was a police officer and one day he was ordered to inspect an excavated well in prison. He hurried over to the deep hole, bent over, and slipped. The following day he was hoisted up, but it was too late. From then on his eldest son had to provide for the family. From an early age, the son worked for India Post, and quickly moved up the ranks. His marriage to my grandmother was arranged, but happy. The couple had ten children: two sons and eight daughters.

'It snowed when your mother was born,' Aunt Jasleen tells me. 'It's one of my first memories. Not much later, we were forced to flee Pakistan. Hindus were tortured and murdered. Millions abandoned their homes, their possessions, and their animals. Our first stop was Kashmir, but when war broke out there, we had to flee again. Again, we went hungry. Again, we were absolutely terrified. Trains full of Hindus were slaughtered. We were lucky — really, really lucky. We ended up in Agra, my parents, all sisters, all brothers.'

My mother's not Indian, but Pakistani.

Aunt Jasleen shows me some photos of the house in Agra. 'This is your mother,' she says, pointing to a girl with long hair.

'What was my mother like as a child?'

'The same as she is now,' Aunt Jasleen replies. 'Every now and then our father would give us a few rupees, but Veena never spent them. When she lent Auntie Sitara money to buy a treat, she charged interest. She charged her own sister!'

The house in Agra is still owned by the family. Auntie Pushpalata, the eldest living sister, resides there now. Aunt Jasleen's things are stored in the house in Agra, too.

'I moved to Ghaziabad without my possessions,' she explains.

I nod again. The transport costs must have been too high.

Aunt Jasleen gets up. 'Let's go and walk Mittu.'

Outside, she ties a flaxen rope around the dog's neck. We go for a walk around the neighbourhood. I give Aunt Jasleen a hand, but she soon extricates herself. Showing affection doesn't come easily to her.

At the entrance to a small park, my aunt stops to inspect the walls. 'A crack,' she says, before taking Mittu into a house where the walls are being erected. Not long after, she re-emerges with a man with a trowel in his hand. He's expected to fix the entrance wall. The man regards the crack reluctantly.

'Why?' he mumbles.

'Why?' my aunt echoes. She takes off her left shoe and starts hitting him with it. 'Here's why!' she yells. 'And here!'

After that, the man shows a little more interest in the crack. He promises Aunt Jasleen he will do something about it.

In the park itself, the gardener is accosted about the weeds. If he doesn't do a better job, my aunt tells him, she's going to phone the local council.

Everybody gets harassed. Aunt Jasleen finds problems wherever she goes, in every nook and cranny.

At the stall where her chauffeur bought bananas the previous day, she complains about the prices. 'Two bananas for five rupees,' Aunt Jasleen exclaims. 'It's daylight robbery.'

The vendor ducks under the counter. I wouldn't be at all surprised if my aunt had brought her rolling pin.

'Show your face if you're man enough,' she commands.

The vendor stays put. From underneath the counter, he urges Aunt Jasleen to remain calm. But she's beside herself. 'I'm throwing away all of your bananas,' she threatens him. 'I used to be unbeatable in the discus circle!'

Aunt Jasleen only calms down when the vendor offers her two free bananas — a settlement that takes at least an hour.

By now I'm numb and not up to any more confrontations. Mittu, however, never tires of tracing circles around her owner. She's the only one who can stick it out with Aunt Jasleen.

'Four bananas for five rupees is a good price,' she says as we walk away, satisfied at last.

I feel a twinge in my body — the beginning of a stomach ache. For a minute, I think it may be down to Aunt Jasleen's spicy food, but back at the big house I don't feel sick. I can't place the shooting pains. Am I homesick? Am I missing my seventeen-month-old son in Italy?

Aunt Jasleen is lying on her bed, watching a film on television. The appliance is faulty, but my aunt reckons it's still better than a husband. I sit down next to her on the bed. I look at her face, at the dark spots under her eyes, the downy hair she has, too. And then I realise what I'm feeling: sadness. It's as if I'm looking at my mother, but without my father, without children; lonely, in a house that hasn't been completed; forever trapped by her pride, sucked deeper and deeper into problems nobody will resolve for her.

Who will take care of her in the future? Who will comb her grey hair when she's no longer capable of doing so herself?

Auntie Sitara told me there was a man in Jasleen's life once. The marriage had been arranged; the two families had come to an agreement. But Jasleen thought the 40,000-rupee dowry her father was giving her was too low. She wanted at least 100,000 rupees. So the wedding was called off, so she fell out with everyone, so she remained alone.

I want to hug her, wrap my arms tightly around her. She's just like my mother, except even more difficult.

Two days later, we drive to Delhi. Aunt Jasleen is taking me to the bazaars of Chandni Chowk. 'We're going shopping!' she exclaims in the car. I hold on to the handrail above the window. There's no greater danger than Delhi traffic. Signs along the side of the road warn that not everybody will make it home. My aunt issues non-stop instructions to the kid behind the wheel. Asked why she doesn't drive herself, she tells me she doesn't have a licence.

'Has it expired?' I ask, naïve as I am, the half-Indian.

'No,' my aunt replies. 'Why would I need a licence when I have a chauffeur?'

Why would my mother need a season ticket when she has a companion pass?

When traffic grinds to a halt, a little boy taps on my window. He does a trick with a hula hoop and asks for money. Behind him, on the hard shoulder, his mother is breastfeeding a baby. She gestures to indicate she's hungry. I'm about to take money from my wallet and hand it to the boy when the car starts moving again. Through the rear window I watch the mother and baby. It makes me want to get out of the car and make just one day in their life a little more bearable: one day without hunger, without thirst, without worries. But I see them everywhere by the side of the road: the barefoot children, the young women with newborn babies, the people who have nothing but their bodies, the people my mother would love to treat to the things we throw away. It's another of her dreams, but none of her dreams come true.

'This is the Red Fort,' my aunt says, and points to the right.

I look at the high red sandstone walls. Tourists queue outside the entrance. We keep driving; Auntie Jasleen has neither season ticket nor companion pass.

In my travel guide I read about all the things I'm missing out on: the green gardens, the marble baths, and the palace of colours that was plundered by the British.

'Stop,' Aunt Jasleen yells. We've reached Chandni Chowk, a boulevard where every square centimetre is contested. Cars are loaded and unloaded in the middle of the road, with the rest of traffic criss-crossing around them. Some cars drive in the wrong direction. In the middle of this hell, my aunt has spotted a parking space.

'Reverse,' she tells the chauffeur.

When I look over my shoulder, I see two rickshaws. The chauffeur also spots them in his rear-view mirror, but he keeps reversing, spurred on by Aunt Jasleen.

The rickshaw riders backpedal a little before gesturing that they can't go any further.

My aunt opens her window and starts yelling. Yes, they *can* go further is what she must be yelling, as the rickshaws retreat a little more. And so they create space for the back part of the car. It's not enough, but we can move a little further back — that's to say, if the stall selling socks and trousers makes way. Again, Aunt Jasleen yells out of her window. Grumbling, the vendor drags his stall behind him, in search of another spot. India, too, is a land of boundless opportunity.

'Right in front of the entrance,' Aunt Jasleen says happily as she gets out of the car.

We enter a bazaar. The place smells of cardamom and cloves, spices my mother always adds to rice. My aunt pauses at each small shop, inquiring after prices before walking off in a huff. 'All crooks,' she says to me. 'Cheats.'

We finally get somewhere at the seventh shop. My aunt nods as the vendor lists his prices. Then she names her own price. A frown appears on the vendor's face — deep grooves. For a moment I fear I may be forced to sit on a sack of cumin until the vendor capitulates. But it doesn't take long for them to reach agreement.

'They know me,' Aunt Jasleen says, and pumps her fist.

In another shop, we buy five kilos of rice. I carry the load on my back.

'Everything is much cheaper here than in Canada,' my aunt exclaims.

Canada?

'Your mother called. She asked us to buy a whole raft of things.'

After taking the rice and spices to the car, we move on to another bazaar. Aunt Jasleen pauses in front of a shop selling toiletries. My attention is drawn to a stack of oblong red boxes: Colgate Super Shakti Dental Cream. It's the toothpaste that chased me off my mother's breast and that I later used to brush my teeth. In fact, I used it throughout my childhood. We must have imported an untold number of tubes into the Netherlands. My aunt asks the vendor how much toothpaste he has in stock.

I walk back and forth between the car and the different bazaars in much the same way that my mother lugged carrier bags home on Den Toom's final opening day. The trunk is filling up with toilet rolls, shaving foam, pans, dishes, trivets, you name it. In India, everything's on special all the time.

Finally, we buy two new suitcases. 'Otherwise you'll have trouble getting everything home on the plane,' Aunt Jasleen says. 'And your mother can never have enough suitcases.'

I nod.

The following day, my kidnapping comes to an end. Aunt Jasleen takes me back to Noida. 'So,' is the first thing she says to her sister, 'did I starve him to death?'

Auntie Sitara takes me in her arms. I've come back in one piece.

'Won't you make us some tea?' Aunt Jasleen asks. I feel a twinge in my stomach.

Auntie Sitara's arms slacken. She lets go of me and makes her way to the kitchen, where she fills a pan with water.

A little later I'm sitting between the mild and the difficult versions of my mother, quietly drinking tea from ABN AMRO mugs.

The bathroom door is closed. 'Uncle is taking a shower,' Auntie Sitara says and smiles.

When my mug is empty, I unload the car together with the chauffeur. My room fills with bags and boxes. I could start a supermarket in the Netherlands.

It's time to say goodbye. We're standing outside, in the hot afternoon sun. Aunt Jasleen shakes my hand, but I pull her close, hug her, and hold her tight. At first she puts up a fight and knocks her head against my chest, but then she relaxes, yields, holds me. Or tries to, anyway. But it's not working. She can't do it. Aunt Jasleen wriggles free and gets in the car. I wonder if I'll ever see her again.

The final few days of my stay are endless summer days. I meditate with Auntie Sitara and Uncle Kakar, and we go for long walks at daybreak. I listen to their stories. My memories of this visit mustn't be mere clouds of smoke.

Then the moment comes for me to leave. The taxi pulls up outside the house. Uncle Kakar helps me with the suitcases: four in total, and all extremely heavy. He hugs me and wishes me a safe journey; he's not coming with me to the airport. With tears in her eyes, Auntie Sitara wraps her arms around me and holds me tight. She kisses me.

'I have to go,' I whisper. 'I have to go back home.'

She doesn't want to let go of me.

AMSTERDAM, it says on the screen above the check-in desk. My heart is in my throat when I place my suitcases on the luggage belt. But the stewardess doesn't sigh. She smiles. There's no such thing as excess weight in India. One by one, the suitcases glide into the belly of Indira Gandhi International Airport. I can go straight to the gate.

In a month's time, my father is coming to the Netherlands for a conference. He's bringing no more than a small carry-on bag with a toothbrush and an article on prostate cancer, because he's supposed to take the Indian stuff back to Canada. Two suitcases.

Why would my mother hire a shipping company when she has my father?

At the check-in desk he'll be confronted with the new luggage restrictions and transfer a couple of things from the suitcases to his small carry-on bag. Not that it will make much of a difference. In a last-ditch effort, my father will hide some of the luggage in his coat. Then, in the men's toilets, he will comb the tufts of hair above his ears and try to get through security with ten kilos of toothpaste.

IN ITALY

From there to here. From Delhi to Amsterdam to Bolzano. To the here and now. My son watches me with wonder in his eyes. Sometimes we are apart longer than we are together. We live in two different countries: my girlfriend and our son in Italy, me in the Netherlands. I'm difficult, too.

'That,' my son says, pointing to a pen. Most things haven't acquired a name yet.

I try to kiss him, but my three-day beard is prickly. He shakes his head: *no kiss.*

'That,' he says again.

'Pen,' I say.

His eyes are smiling. Language is a shimmering layer over things, like powdery snow. Not long now and everything will be covered.

This *covering* — it just happens; there's not even any need for wind. We'll be buried while we're sitting here, every word a flake. I can't help it, although

I know the time has come for me to say something about myself, to take off my cardigan and leave my shoes in the hallway.

'Daddy,' my son says. The word whirls down on me.

'Don't be afraid,' I whisper. 'We don't have to hide.'

He smells sweet: chamomile, with just a hint of mother's milk. He's still breastfed before bed. He's allowed to drink a whole month longer than I was back in the day. Perhaps I should have brought a tube of toothpaste with me to Italy. Instead I bought him some small wooden elephants. But he doesn't think much of the animals and has pushed them away.

'That,' he says, pointing to the pen again. He slides off my lap and toddles over to the cabinet with the pen on top. He tries, but can't reach it. He looks as if he's dancing on tip-toe. It looks funny — a little Van der Kwast with wooden hips.

I walk over to my son and lift him up. He snatches at the pen with his tiny fingers. Before I know it, he has a blue line across his face. When he sticks the pen into his mouth, I pull it out of his hand. His face crumples and he starts crying. 'Mama,' he screeches. 'Mama, mama, mama.' A snowstorm of words.

She swoops him up into her arms to comfort him. His tears dry, and he's soon smiling again.

'That,' he also says to his mother, pointing to the pen I'm holding in my right hand. '*That.*'

'You should write something for him.'

I think of the magical words Saint-Exupéry wrote somewhere: *Ah, I owe you a page, Mademoiselle.*

This final page is for my son, my first-born, my pride. For you.

I lift my hand up in the air and write with the pen: *You could spend your whole life on one and the same piece of land, and yet could see an extraordinary amount. Everything depends on your curiosity and perception.*

'What are you writing?'

'A line by Konstantin Paustovsky.' And in your ear I whisper: 'Look closely, and you'll see things that aren't there.' Your eyes grow bigger. *More*, they seem to be saying.

'No quotes,' your mother says. 'Something of your own …'

Never marry an Indian woman, I write in the air, but immediately blow away the words.

You turn your head and look outside, where the sun is shining. You don't want advice. You want to discover everything for yourself.

I catch your attention by writing frantically — long, whirling ribbons. Halfway through a sentence, you look at the pen in my hand that writes: … *takes the lift down and heads to the airport — without suitcases, without a rolling pin. Everybody has seen you: Ashirwad, Johan, my father. Everybody that is, except my mother. She's never held you in her arms, never sung for you. 'Chandaa maama door ke, puye pakaayen boor ke': a lullaby about the moon refusing to eat its biscuit. That's all I know about* it, *because I only understand my mother when she swears in Hindi.*

A frown appears on your forehead. This isn't right, and I know it.

She gets on the plane and crosses the ocean. Her snoring is so loud, the pilots think the engine's broken. But the plane doesn't crash, and once it's touched down safely in Italy your grandma takes the train to Bolzano. And she walks all the way from the station to our house, because she thinks the taxi is too expensive.

You look entranced, as if you can see what I'm writing: the taxi driver locking his door and rolling up his window as fast as he can.

Then Mama Tandoori turns up on the doorstep. Her finger reaches for the doorbell.

'Oh,' I hear from your mouth, and suddenly you look frightened, as if you're about to burst into tears and tantrums.

Don't be afraid, I write. *We don't have to hide.*

We walk to the door. You go in front, because you want to push down the door handle. You can just reach it with your fingers. Sometimes you open the door and it's me standing outside. Sometimes there's nobody. This time the door opens and you look through the crack with curious, expectant eyes.